# RAG D

by
## Dougie Wilson

*For*
*Bill and Woody and Ian*

# Prologue

## 1979

Chilly, low, late-October sun cast long shadows. At short notice, Kim Jae-Gyu decided he would host a banquet that evening. This was nothing unusual. He threw maybe ten of them every month. The guest lists were calculated to help him gauge the *zeitgeist* at least, more often, tongues loosened by *soju* and fine Italian wines, to glean concrete information. In the midst of popular uprisings in Busan and Masan, which were bound to spread to all major cities, this was a pressing concern.

He flicked on the TV. KBS. President Park Chung Hee was cutting a ribbon at the opening of a new KBSTV transmitting station in Dongjin. The President would be invited that evening, as would, more importantly, the man at his right hand on the screen, the bodyguard, as Mr. Kim still considered him, Cha Ji-Chul. There would be the usual girls, he had two in mind already, and you didn't refuse an invitation from the Agency, not if you knew what was good for you. And Chief Secretary Kim Gye-won would be there. To keep the atmosphere light, if nothing else, which might well prove necessary.

He should be in Dongjin. As Director of the KCIA, it was his TV station, after all, totally under his control. But such was the brutish parvenu Cha's current influence, Mr. Kim had found himself banned from riding in the presidential helicopter. He had excused himself from the trip with as much *sang-froid* as he could muster.

Having brought the domestic staff up to speed and given instructions to issue the invitations, he lay down in his room and

1

reaching into the drawer of his bedside table, removed the semi-automatic Walther PPK and checked it was loaded. He smiled to himself. James Bond's gun, a good weapon for a spook on a mission. Like the old days.

# 1

A rainbow arched over Morvern. Against the odds, it was trying its best to be a nice day. On the shore of Loch Sunart, a small fire nestled in the rocks, heating a pot of water. A large creature broke the silence and the surface of the waves. A wet fox left its sniffing of the provisions and hot-tailed it into the trees. Dave Bruce reared up with the grace of a pale walrus and flailed through the seaweed to the shore. Throwing on his clothes, he scrambled shivering to the fire, put more sticks on in a vain attempt to get dry. Was there any chance of the water becoming warm enough to make a decent cup of coffee? Any danger of the tent drying off enough before he struck camp to be not completely mildewed the next time he used it? What were the odds on Dagenham's Disgrace, a sky-blue Mk. 1 Ford Escort, making it even as far as the Corran Ferry?

Following the untimely collapse of DB Sounds, he should be signing on in approximately three hours, so that was the weekend fucked. But… yes, he still had fifteen pounds in his jeans, the sorry remains of the derisory sum he'd got for selling off his entire album stock. Bastards. Still, there you go. It would be enough for petrol back home and the full Scottish in Spean Bridge, and who gave a shite anyway. The music was all in his head and it was beautiful here, it cleansed your soul just sitting hunched over the fire and being a part of it all. Two cormorants glided in inches above the water, landed, floated serenely, and were swallowed by the rippling loch.

# 2

Freezing har rolled in off the sea like it was in a hurry to make everybody's life miserable. There was no reason for Bob McMillan to have woken this early. No sense to it at all. People with work to go to might be getting up about now, but, Jesus, it was only quarter past seven, and another long day of nothing sprawled out ahead. It had been after three when he'd got to his bed, worse for wear. He looked from his pillow at the devastation which was his bijou boudoir and struggled to list the available options. He could try to get back to sleep. Nah. He had to pish, and replace it with a quart or so of liquid in the other end. How much had he drunk the previous night? He gave up around the darts game in the Lochside, when he'd hit the old wifie's dog with an unfortunate rebound. And then, oh Jesus Christ Almighty, back at that guy Igor's flat, the biker... his mind filled with abject horror... Kim Anderson... gorgeous, sexy Kim Anderson... the glass misted over... he remembered the T-shirt, in particular the breasts beneath it... but what had he said, what had he done?... nothing specific came to him, just an overwhelming unease. He shuddered, and turned his attention to immediate physical problems. Wrapping the quilt around him, he staggered to his feet, breath steamy in the chill as he crossed the sticky carpet. The merry sound of cascading water accompanied a joyful wave of relief, tempered by the sight of the haggard wreck which stared at him from the mirror. From the nearby shore the foghorn brayed mournful at the blind sea. Strategy? As he drank from the tap, he rejected the idea of a return to bed. Too cold. Too damp. Shuffled into the sitting room which also served as his bedroom. No bloody matches! The fourth run from the cooker was the successful one, the incendiary material, an ancient rolled-up copy of the *Press and Journal* (North-East Night Out Ends in Tragedy, and, on the B-side, Dismal Dons in Dens Debacle). Like a torch bearer in

4

the Obscene Olympics, the stained quilt billowing behind him, Bob dived at the greasy gas fire just as the flames scorched his hand. The paper blazed on the carpet. The gas hissed. Returning from the kitchen with a fish slice, he spooned the remains of the flickering newsprint towards the fire. The words "Good Morning Aberdeen" were consumed, a fireball licked out at him, and the radiator reverted serenely to its usual half-arsed mode of operation. He beat out the remaining embers with his spatula and settled shivering on the floor. He conjured up a vision of coffee, fruit juice, kippers, rowies, butter, jam. The shop would be open in half an hour. He pulled a pair of clammy jeans towards him. 27p. Realistically rolls. And he could probably persuade Mr. Aziz to sell him a couple of loose eggs. Magic. Life was sweet. The foghorn moaned.

# 3

Scotland stirred. Out on the streets, scaffies clattered bins to rouse those tempted by a lie-in this cold morning. Aziz Ibrahim reflected that only yesterday, it seemed, he was a much younger man who could shift all these newspapers without getting out of breath. Holding the shop door open with his arse, he hoyed them on to the ice cream freezer and, taking a slug from a hot mug of tea, began to cut open the stacks and put them on display. And there she was on the front page of the *Scottish Daily Express*. The patron saint of the small businessman. He kissed the image, as another entrepreneur in the western schemes of town saluted her on leaving his bedroom.

The lucky ones woke up with their loved ones. Elsewhere in the city: a man from the printing trade thanked the lord it was Friday, while his wife took stock of how she felt and how long she could conceal it and made a mental note to put aside the usual £20 from her wage packet that evening; a long-haired, bearded young man named Ian Gordon boosted his already high self-esteem by opening his eyes and registering the shock of blonde hair on the pillow next to his, and the frankly sensational body attached to it; a small girl, on hearing the sound of an approaching vehicle, identified it correctly and made herself scarce while two uniformed men woke her companion before moving him on.

In Peterhead the racket of two infants roused a young woman not yet accustomed to waking up alone, who reached automatically for the happy pills and a fag. In West Lothian, a father handed his daughter a fiver. "It's oor wee secret, eh?" She was already planning the vendetta. The knife was sharp and the dug might get some unexpected treats tonight.

The nation's capital found a ginger young man still dreaming, of aquatic pursuits and California Girls, and its largest metropolis could similarly do nothing to pique the interest for the time being of a youth whose intake of recreational pharma the previous evening promised to keep him exactly where he was for the foreseeable.

Meanwhile, at Nice Airport, the passport clerk reflected that the photograph of *la rousse* did not do her justice. *"Vous allez ou, mademoiselle?"*

*"Londres, et ensuite Edimbourg."*

*"Ecossaise, hein?"*

*"Oui."*

*"Bon voyage, chérie."*

# 4

The fish-slice was working well. Bob McMillan flipped two fried eggs into warm rolls, shook salt and an ancient bottle of tomato ketchup at his breakfast, and hurried back to the living room, which was getting warm enough for penguins. He switched on the radio and listened for some thirty seconds to some desperate cheerful bastard before thinking better of it. Music, though, was what the occasion demanded. He cursed Dave for selling the finest album collection ever and turned to his own. He'd listened to them all a thousand times. Bowie. He grinned. She loved the Thin White Soul Boy Leper Messiah Chameleon Comedian Corinthian Caricature Fucker unconditionally whatever he chose to show up as. Bob wondered what she was doing now. Morag McPherson. Morag McPhabulous, Morag McPhun, Morag McPhantastic. Morag McPhucking-Gorgeous. The four months they had spent together seemed like a dream now. But it had really happened. He had photographic evidence and a broken heart. He'd written shite poetry, the full Magilla. She had vanished as quickly as she had appeared, off to the Cote d'Azur with some French student, his alleged mate. Tall, dark, and devious. Xavier. From that day, Bob had never trusted anyone whose name began with an X. He had received a letter from Cannes. She hadn't even expressed any regret. Bob had replied thus:

'As an avid viewer of the Morag McPhilthy Show. I must say I found last week's episode boring and predictable. Wouldn't it have been more interesting if she'd gone off with the ugly Scottish dwarf (whose name escapes me)?

Yours truly,
Wee Bobby McPillock
Strathhaggis, Isle of Shite'

He put the record on, the train started, and he lay on his back and finished the baps, dripping runny egg on his face. The last few years had left him with a degree of sorts from the University of Edinburgh, a sketchy knowledge of metaphysical poetry and debts up to his ears. And without the girl. His thoughts led him to a makeshift bookcase of scaff boards and beer tins, from which he extracted *The Literature of Renaissance England*. He flicked idly through the pages and the book fell open at "Doctor Faustus". In the brave new world of the psycho swivel-eyed Gorgon he might get a fiver for his soul these days.

Bob worked his way through the Marlowe, accompanying his reading with a catholic musical selection. The previous evening's revelry was catching up with him as he turned to the final page. He crawled over to the bed and kicked off his trainers. He would read the last few lines in his scratcher. He burrowed under the quilt, tried to force his blurring mind to make sense of a footnote, and in seconds his eyes were closed and his breathing deep and even.

Several hours later a key turned in the door of the flat. A large young man entered the small entrance hall, then opened the door to the room where Bob McMillan slept. A sweltering wave hit him. It was like disembarking from an aeroplane in the tropics. He looked around at the dirty plates and mugs, the scattered books, periodicals and vinyl, at the pile of ashes in front of the red-hot gas fire. Shaking his head, he went over, turned it off, checked with disapproval the strewn sleeveless records, picked up a single, and having ascertained that it hadn't melted, stuck on "Gangsters" loud.

The fat youth spoke. "Himmin. Fit's 'e scoop here?" Bob McMillan groaned and rolled over. "Are you in league wi' British Gas or are you jist so hungry yer tryin tae cook yersel?"

Indistinct words came from beneath the quilt. "Giwayaraj. Smaberoom. Leevmalane."

"It may be your bedroom, buddy boy, but it's also my livin room, and it's *oor* gas bill. Jesus. Fit a state tae get intil. Div you wint a cup ay tea?"

Bob's head poked out of the side of the bed. "D'ye hiv tea? Magic!"

"Na. I wis jist bein wildly optimistic and thinkin you maybe hidnae used it a'."

Bob groaned again, and questioned the intruder. "How wis the Hielans?"

"Still there, Bobby min. Fit's happenin?"

"Cannae remimber. Got howlin last night."

"Uh-huh."

"Onythin strange oot there?"

"Dictator ay South Korea's got himsel assassinated."

"Careless! Still, death tae all tyrants, eh. Car gan a'right?"

"Kindae. Problem wi' the electrics."

"Fit's up wi' 'em?"

"Fucked."

"Got back OK, though."

"Na, ran out ay juice oot by Kintore. Hid tae hitch it in. Boy gave me a lift right tae 'e door. Tree surgeon. Nivver even kent 'at wis an option."

"So I tak it you're stoney an' a', David?"

"Nae quite. I've took the precaution ay keepin a fiver back for some refreshments later on."

"You're 'e boy for me, Brucie. Hero ay the Soviet Union, 3rd class. Here, you could've got some petrol for 'e motor wi' 'at."

"Life's too short, min. One must try tae retain a sense ay proportion. Onywey, 'e fuel gauge disnae work ony mair. I thought I'd be OK, and besides, if I'd switched her aff tae fill her up there was nae guarantee she wid've stairted again."

"It's a credit tae British engineerin, 'at vehicle."

"Och aye, maks you proud."

"Well, it wis a heroic act ay self-sacrifice, and don't think it isnae appreciated. God's watchin your every move, Dave, and I should imagine he's pretty damn impressed."

"Right, here's 'e plan. I'm gonnae tak a bath. Meanwhile I entrust you wi' 'is five-spot tae get us wir tea in 'e maist economical wye ye ken how."

"It's nivver 'at time, is it?"

"Five fifty-one and a half. 'E big hand is obscurin Goofy's puss."

"Jesus."

Dave handed the money to the still recumbent Bob McMillan, exited to the bathroom and could be heard taking his friend's name in vain. "McMillan! C'm'ere!"

"Fit's up?"

"You've hid a' my Vidal Sassoon, ya raj." Dave re-entered, incensed.

"Oh, aye."

"Dinnae jist say, 'Oh, aye'. Fit am I gonnae wash my hair wi'?"

"Soap?"

"I dinnae believe 'is!"

"Vanity's a terrible thing, Fatman. Leave us some het watter, will ye. Onywey, 'e night, far we gan?"

"Albyn."

"The Albyn? Are you feelin a'right?"

"Nivver better, Robert. I sense you may have an objection to my plan."

"Mair than one. Firstly, it's really expensive and efter I've got wir tea we've got, fit, £3 to spend and also it's at the ither end ay toon. How do you propose we get there?"

"*A pied.*"

"Eh?"

"We'll hoof it."

"I understood the French, Brucie, the 'Eh' wis meant tae convey incredulity."

"Fit's 'e metter wi' ye? It's a fine night." Bob looked hopelessly out at the dense grey drizzle. "Have faith, my son", said Dave with an expansive gesture as he exited towards the bathroom, "and get us shampoo while yer oot."

Bob's protests were cut short by the slamming of the bathroom door and Dave singing 'King Creole' as the plumbing burst into life, harmonising nicely with the foghorn.

# 5

The tide was coming in across the broad beach and had been for some time. Sheets of freezing rain gusted over the sand. And yet still he lay motionless amongst the seaweed and debris. She shook him, but there was no response. She took shelter and observed.

# 6

As they made their way down towards the river in silence, brisk against the weather, Dave Bruce seemed distracted, even upset. This was not normal. Bob confronted the issue.

"Nae trace ay yer usual sunny disposition 'is evenin, big man. Fit's on your mind?"

"Nithin."

"Na. There's somethin. I can tell. Fit're ye thinkin aboot 'is very second?"

"Kim Anderson's knockers."

"You're quite shallow, really, are you, Dave?"

"Och ay. 'Ere are deeper puddles, min."

"Fuck me, 'at's nae rain, 'at's sleet."

"Not at all. It's a fine enough evenin. Fit wye are you in such a fool mood?"

"I'm nae. Jist makkin a meteorological observation. It's only fuckin October, fuck's sake." Bob pulled his jacket tight around him. His thoughts turned to football. They walked on in silence till they'd crossed the bridge. "Ken 'is, I never thought I'd forgive Fergie for drappin 'e King, but I believe I jist hiv."

"Doubt not the wisdom of his ways, Bob, for he is not as ither men are. Onywey, at 'e risk ay bein controversial, Stevie Archibald, even better 'an wee Joey. I dinnae even ken if he's drapped him as such, I think he's injured. They at hame 'e morn?"

"Na, Easter Road, min."

"Couldnae afford it in ony case."

"You know, Dave, beatin 'e Hun is always great, obviously, because they are the physical manifestation ay pure evil stalkin 'e face ay 'e planet, but beatin Celtic, min, at Parkheid! Mind fan we first started gan tae Pittodrie, those Celtic teams, man. The Lisbon Lions, and then Dalglish and Macari and McGrain, they had poetry, they were legendary. Jimmy Johnstone, fuck's sake. In Lisbon he's up against the Inter Milan defence, and they're like Roman gods, one ay them's gan oot wi' Gina Lollobrigida, fuck's sake, and the wee man looks like he's got some kindae vitamin deficiency, complexion like a bottle ay milk, and it's nae contest, he hisnae got a chunce, except he's got the magic and they hivnae, and they cannae get the ba' aff him, they cannae even fuckin kick him, he's ower fly for 'em, he's makkin monkeys ay 'em, and there's Jock Stein on the sidelines, an' 'at, and we did 'at tae them. For Jinky and Stein, read Gordon and Fergie. We're on wir wye, man, that'll be us in a few years."

"One step at a time, Bobby, they hivnae even won 'e League yet."

"I do believe they're goin tae, Brucie."

"Ken 'is, I think you might be right."

In the chill, grey dusk at the end of the harbour, they started dancing.

# 7

Finally, wet and cold, Bob and Dave found themselves at Queen's Cross and entered the Albyn, surrounding themselves with the best shot at beautiful people that the Granite City could manage. Almost immediately the previous night was brought into sharp focus. As they waited to get served the lovely Kim Anderson, Aberdeen's answer to Brigitte Bardot, came past with an almost equally gorgeous mate. Dave refrained from actually drooling. He spoke, initially to Bob.

"Dear me, but 'at quine has a big chest... Good evening, Kimberley."

"My name's nae Kimberley, it's jist Kim."

"Like the assassin?"

"Eh? Hiv you got the £100, Bobby?"

Bob was genuinely confused. "Fit?"

"The £100 you said you'd gie me if I slept wi' you." And she crossed the bar.

Dave grinned. "You charmin devil, Robert."

Everything came back to Bob. Reddening like a traffic light, he interrupted Dave's amusement. "Ye ken she's gan oot wi' 'e boy there."

"Fit boy?"

"'E big ape 'at's jist pit his tongue doon her throat. Igor, 'e biker."

"That is jist a criminal waste, man."

"'E lassie's panderin tae a' her basest instincts."

Shaking his head, Dave turned to the barman. "Two pints ay your cheapest lager, please."

"We dinnae sell cheap lager."

"Christ, hiv you nae got a discount on ony o' them?"

A lad in a broadly pin-striped suit had entered the establishment. His features resembled those of a ferret, and indeed, he was familiarly referred to in those terms. He came up behind Dave Bruce and slapped him heartily between the shoulder blades.

"Fuck me, Fatman, I hinna seen you in donkeys!"

"Aye, Ferret. Fit like?"

"Nivver better. Rakin it in, min."

He reached a hand in front of Dave.

"Excuse my manners. We hinna been introduced."

Dave did the honours. "Bob McMillan, Ferret. Ferret, Bob McMillan."

"Dinnae listen tae him. 'E name's Chris, Chris Innes. So you're Bob McMillan. Heard a lot ay good things about you, my friend. Been at university, am I right? I respect that. Education, man, it's the wye forward. I could use a bright spark like you in the organisation. You too, David. We need tae talk. Fit are you guys drinkin?"

He took their order and pushed in to the bar.

"Fit the fuck?" inquired Bob.

"Lives next door tae ma cousin Gogs in Mastrick. Chuncer. Still. Gift horse. Choppers. Do not inspect too closely. Check her!"

"She's tiny, Dave."

"Perfectly formed, though."

"It'd be a bit ay a Rottweiler/Chihuahua thing, eh? Fit wid yer bairns be like?"

"I sometimes think you can extract the magic from almost any situation."

"I dae ma best. D'ye think Kim Anderson's really 'at blonde?"

"Naaa. Naebody's 'at blonde. Nae even Swedish blondes 'n'at."

"Fit aboot her tits?"

"How do you mean? D'ye think they may hiv been enhanced in some way? Naa, she's fae Tilly, far wid she get 'e money for that fae?"

"Fae ony one ay us, really. She'd only hiv tae ask."

"True", Dave sighed and his eyes glazed over as he stared at her, "and yet I feel she is Mother Nature's child."

"Ayyye."

Ferret returned with drinks. "Sorry tae hear aboot 'e shop, Dave."

Dave shrugged. "Easy come 'n'at, Ferret."

"So, you loons workin?"

"Na."

"Excellent news! I think I may have openins in the organisation."

"Fit organisation?"

"Hiv ye nae heard? Innes International Incorporated. There was a thing aboot me in the *Evenin Express*."

"Congratulations."

"Aye, man, I'm on my wye, and I'd feel good if you guys were ridin 'e wave wi' me."

Bob was sceptical. "So, fit sphere dis I.I.I. operate in chiefly, Christopher?"

"Weel, Bob, oor main area ay expertise is in support for the ile industry, but I'm diversifyin a' the time. For instance, I think I might hiv a niche for you, David, in wir hearin aid division. Yeah. Sales. I think you could be dynamite."

"I think he's got somethin there, Dave," added Bob helpfully. "You've aye hid quite a loud voice."

"So this would be, like, a real job, Ferret," inquired Dave, "wi' money?"

"Three grand a year basic, same again easy in commission, plus I could see a man like you climbin the corporate ladder like a wee monkey."

In spite of himself, Dave heard himself say, "Fan wid I start?"

"Morn's morn."

"Fit? On a Setterday?"

"Och aye, Dave. Best time for catchin 'e deef folk in. We work hard and we play hard. Now, you, Bob, I have mair ay a problem wi'. Overqualified, you see. But I'll hae a think. Dinnae accept nithin else till you've talked tae me. Dave, here's ma caird. Nine o'clock at HQ 'e morn. Now, I think this calls for shumpers." And he was off to the bar again.

Dave and Bob looked at one another.

Dave spoke first, "Did I jist...?"

"Looks 'at wye, Dave."

And the evening proceeded merrily enough, given that they were obliged to spend it in the company of their new benefactor, who, fair play to him, kept a kaleidoscope of drinks coming all night, until, inspired and bold, he declared that Kim Anderson would be a fitting consort to stand by him at the head of his new business empire. The lads concurred that it would be churlish of her not to consider such a magnanimous offer, and sat back to watch developments as he staggered over and planted himself squarely between her and the big scary motorcyclist. It was gripping viewing, and remarkable in that it was several minutes before young Christopher Innes was asked to step outside, never to return.

# 8

8 a.m., Saturday morning. Bob McMillan was woken by Dave entering the sitting room in a suit.

"Fuck me. Fa's deid, Fatman?"

"Fuck off."

"You're nae gonnae get far in 'e cut and thrust ay the modern corporate world wi' that attitude."

"Fuck off."

"Or wi' that suit come tae that."

"Fuck off. It's a' been doonhill for Burton's the Tailors since they came up wi' 'is wee beauty. 'E deef fowk'll fuckin lap it up, min."

"Deef, nae blind, Davie. You oot 'e night?"

"Na. Unless you plan tae pawn 'e Fabergé eggs, we're skint. I'm awa roon ma Ma's efter work. I'll probably see you Monday night. Manny's comin for 'e rent 'e day, mind."

"Shite!"

"See ya later."

"Whoa! How am I meant tae pye him. I hinna got nae cash. You're the one wi' a job."

But it was too late. Dave Bruce had left the building.

Bob felt like shite, unprepared to face his public. He badly needed to sleep this one off. But David was not wrong. Today was the day the imaginary rent was due. And the boy could show up any time – starting from right now. Despite the cosy comfort of his bed, the uneasy feeling in his guts and the splitting headache brought on by the fiendish and outlandish diversity of refreshments Ferret had insisted on them sampling, there was nothing for it. He needed to vacate the premises sharpish. Rain lashed against the window. If he was to stay warm, get fed, and maybe even find a temporary solution to the cashflow problem then it was time to set the controls for Chateau McMillan. He threw on some clothes, brushed his teeth, put as much dirty washing into as many plastic bags as he could carry and walked out into the weather. As he reached the end of the street he looked back to see the landlord getting out of his car. Quickening his pace, he disappeared round the corner.

# 9

Dave Bruce had not looked carefully at Ferret's business card until they had parted company the previous evening. Had he done so, he would have noted that the address of Innes International Incorporated was next to his cousin Gogs's place. He got off the 23 bus in good time and took the familiar stroll down the Lang Stracht until he turned the corner into Ferret's road, and, as he did so, exactly what he didn't want to happen came to pass. Gogs emerged from his close on to the pavement and turned towards him.

"Davie, man! Fit like? Fit ye daein' here?"

"Dinnae ask."

"I'd ask you in, but I'm a bittie late for work. My ma and da's there though. Awa in aboot and see 'em. Kettle's jist biled. Seriously, though, man, fit brings ye up 'is wye?"

"Workin'. First day."

"Ye got a job! Congratulations! Fit ye daein?"

"Ach, it's maistly support work for the ile."

"There's nithin' doon here, min. Industrial estate's 'at wye… Oh, Christ, you're nae, are you…?"

"Fit?"

"Naaa, you're nae 'at feel, are ye? Tell me you're nae workin for Ferret."

Dave's silence was interpreted correctly. Gogs burst into a peal of hearty laughter. "Listen, I've got tae scoot, min. 'Is is fuckin priceless. Wait till I tell 'e boys at work. Good luck, Davie loon. Fit's he got you sellin?"

"Hearin aids."

Gogs's laughter actually got louder as he disappeared round the corner.

With a heart suddenly heavy, Dave made his way into the close and up the stairs to the top floor. A stained mattress with scorch marks was propped against the wall outside Ferret's front door. A huge scabby cat that looked like it could take down an antelope but was instead ripping its way into a rubbish bag turned and hissed at his approach before backing into a corner, hackles raised. Dave pushed the bell. It obviously didn't work. He knocked. A retching cough announced the approach of an inhabitant. Ferret's ma opened the door, a fag hanging from her lips.

"You must be Mr. Bruce."

"Ay, I'm Dave, Mrs. Innes. We've met before. I'm Mrs. Cooper fae next door's nephew."

"Come through to reception and take a seat. Mr. Innes will see you shortly."

He followed her through into the living room. It was hard to put your finger on what the cocktail of aromas was, but you could definitely file it under "unpleasant". She indicated a sofa that had seen happier days. He pushed aside a pile of washing waiting to be ironed and sat down. The coffee table was festooned with half-drunk tea mugs, full ashtrays, a partly-consumed sandwich in the process of decomposition, an enormous bowl of similarly mature Cattomeat, and copies of Forbes Magazine, Time and The Economist. A fat dog fixed him with a baleful gaze and farted. Mrs. Innes took her seat behind a desk piled high with random papers and pressed an intercom.

"Mr. Bruce to see you, Mr. Innes."

Footsteps in the lobby and the closing of a door. From the next room the unmistakeable sounds of defaecation.

"So how's things, Mrs. Innes?"

The phone rang. She was on it like a shot. "Innes International Incorporated. How may I direct your call?... I'm sorry, he's currently in a meeting... Uh-huh... Is that right?... Well, I can assure you that 'e cheque wis sent last wik... Well I can assure you that it wis sent last wik... Well, I can assure you that it wis sent last wik... I dinnae hiv tae tolerate language like 'at... Are you fuckin threatenin me... Well, let *me* tell *you* that all our calls are recorded and I am now in a position to sue you for threatenin behaviour and breach ay contract... Aye, you dae that, see if I fuckin care." She replaced the receiver decisively and smiled over at Dave. "He'll be with you shortly."

The toilet flushed and Ferret entered the room with a broad smile, his hand outstretched. "David, David, David, good to see you, my friend." Dave had heard no sounds of hand-washing, but took the proffered handshake as heartily as he could manage. Ferret was wearing a Rangers football strip he had obviously slept in, and his two shiners and multiple abrasions indicated that his previous evening's *contretemps* with Igor had gone more or less to form. He turned to his mother. "Fa wis 'at on 'e phone?"

"Billy Simpson. Hiv you pyed him?"

"Aye, that'll be right! Hold my calls, Mrs. Innes. Come on through to the office, David."

Ferret took a seat at a school desk wedged in at the end of his unmade bed. For want of an alternative Dave sat on the bed. Aside from a completely blank year planner, the room's decoration was devoted to Rangers football club, naked women and a large portrait of the prime minister, preparing to eviscerate a pauper while Keith Joseph sat on their head, by the look in her bulging eyes.

"Nivver kent you were a Hun, Ferret."

"Please, call me Christopher. Oh, aye. True Blue Loyal, me. No surrender, eh? Da tell me you support 'e Sheepshaggers."

"Cuffed you bastards 'e last couple ay times."

"Flash in the pan, I assure you. Onywey, tae business. As I mentioned last night, I'd like you tae tak chairge ay my hearin aids division. I've identified maist ay 'e people in 'e North-East 'at are corn beef. We've done a mail shot. So a' you've got tae dae is show up on their doorsteps and shift 'e product."

"Do deef people nae normally hiv hearin aids already?"

"Aye, but nae like these. 'E trick is tae play on folk's vanity. These things are fuckin tiny, man. And transparent. You hardly notice fan 'e deef boy's wearin it."

"And do they work?"

"Do they shite. Fuck's sake, fatman, it's nae like I'm giein' a guarantee wi' them." He handed Dave some loose sheets of paper and a small carrier bag. "'At's yer addresses and yer samples. £99.99 a shottie. Batteries not included. Cash if you

27

can, but I'll tak cheques if I hiv til. On you go."

"Haud on. How do I get tae these places? My motor's fucked."

"I'd start your transport expense account 'e day, but, cashflow being as it is, I'd just dae the anes aroon here for noo. Now, I'm sorry, Dave, I've another meeting. Go get 'em, Tiger!"

# 10

Mid-Saturday morning found Bob at the parental home. He sat at the kitchen table. His mother, out of breath, brought him a cup of tea and a plate of biscuits, then climbed back on a precarious stool and continued cleaning cupboards. She turned to him. "How's David?"

"Still consumin his own weight in snack foods weekly."

"Ay, they're an affa femmly for eatin, yon. The shoppin bills must be nae real. I blame his grunny. She made affa fine stovies. Jean couldnae get enough ay them."

"She's a fair size ay a wumman, Mrs. Bruce, you'd hiv tae say."

"Ay, but she's gey couthy, Jean. I like her fine."

"A merry quip never far from her lips, right enough."

"So, fit ye daein' wi' yersel, loon?"

"Trying tae tap money aff Roddy."

"You'll be lucky. I've made 'at my life's mission, but it's a sair fecht. Ye heard fae yon quine?"

"Naaa."

"Coorse heilan' bitch."

"Mother, you're spikkin' ay the woman I love."

"There's twa types ay men, Robert. The coorse eens and the

stupit eens. There's nane ay yiz wise. At least you're nae coorse. Fit ye needing 'e money for?"

"Rent."

"Ye ken fine ye can bide here. Ye dinnae hiv tae pye rint."

"And therein lies my only hope. Roddy is caught in the horns of a dilemma. Either he helps me out or he runs the risk of me movin back in here."

"Your da would be delighted tae hae you back."

"Definitions of delight. Roddy McMillan being faced wi' a larger weekly household expenditure. Close, but, sorry, disnae mak it tae 'e Hall ay Fame."

"He disnae think ay it like that."

"He fuckin dis. You can practically hear the beads on the abacus whizzin."

"Your language nivver used to be sae fool afore ye wint tae Edinburgh."

"Aye, it wis. I jist made mair effort then."

"You've nae reason to be scunnert, ken 'at. You've got far mair gan for you than me or your da ivver hid."

"Don't fret yourself, Mamma. It's just a spot of existential angst."

"We nivver hid 'is problem wi' your sister, ken."

"Kathy is married tae a psycho prison warder that's left her, which is a good thing, by the way, except he's left her livin in Peterheid wi' twa bairns she nivver winted in 'e first place and her life for 'e next twinty years is taken care o', thank you very much, as long as 'e doc can keep 'e pills comin. So dinnae spik aboot fit might happen wi' me, because she's twice as clever as I ivver wis. She jist did fit wis expectit ay her, eh?"

Bob's mum's back was turned to him, but he could tell she was crying. She looked frail, defeated, he thought.

"I'm sorry, ma. I'm full ay shite. Ye ken I love yiz a'."

"Listen, sometimes you dinnae mak 'e right choices, but life disnae stop while ye sort it oot. It just keeps right on gan, an' nine times oot ay ten it's nae whit ye would have chosen, but ye've got to be happy, Robert. Fit's 'e alternative?"

"I'll awa and pit 'e squeeze on Roddy again, eh?"

"Fuck off."

"Mother?"

"You heard me." She came back in with her coat. "There's denner for you and yer da in the oven. Jist need tae heat it up. I'm awa doon toon." For as long as Bob could remember, you could set your watch by his mother's mystery Saturday schedule. She never worked on a weekend, and was always back early in the afternoon. It was taken as read and, if anyone was going to question what she got up to, they would have done so years ago. Too late now.

# 11

Bob had stuck around on Saturday and endured the chilly atmosphere long enough to roast his heid in front of the open fire and *World of Sport*, get two square meals and all his clothes washed and ironed. Eventually it got late enough for him to risk a return to the flat.

A note awaited him in large, angry capitals:

CAME TODAY FOR RENT AS AGREED! NOBODY HOME! WILL BE HERE AGAIN TOMORROW AND THERE HAD BETTER BE SOMEBODY IN! THE PLACE IS A COWP! PLEASE CLEAN IT UP! IT IS A HEALTH HAZARD! YOU ARE ON YOUR FINAL WARNING! THIS IS NOT A JOKE!

Bob set the alarm for early and collapsed into bed.

Sunday morning broke with less rain but with a wind in a hurry to get out of Siberia so it could bug people's happiness right across the North-East of Scotland. With no clear plan except avoidance of his financial responsibilities, Bob put on several layers of clothes, went out the front door and started walking. He could visit some friends. No, he couldn't. Not yet, anyway, it was half past eight on a Sunday morning. In any case, he didn't feel even slightly sociable. A foul scunner hung over him like a black cloud. Boring old fucking Ab on a dreich Sunday. You could almost feel the Presbyterianism gripping you by the throat and squeezing the life out of you. Without even the inconvenience of going to the kirk.

So he walked. Across Balnagask golf course to the lighthouse via the Battery, round Nigg Bay, over Tullos Hill and back down to the river by the jail. Into town, up Union Street all the way and further out, past Queen's Cross and the Albyn again, and further out, his mind blank, all the way to Hazlehead. Kids on horses, men playing golf, families with dogs, people with lives. He took them all in. He didn't want to be like them, he didn't even understand how you became like them. Their happiness, their normality, was nipping his heid. He rose from the wet grass and headed back into town.

At the bottom of Union Street he walked into the broad expanse of the Castlegate. Some old jakie was lying on the pavement eating a discarded fish supper straight out of the gutter. Seagulls circled screaming above him, furious at the breach of etiquette. Bob took a seat on the steps of the Mercat Cross to observe developments. If the birds had worked as a team there would have been no problem. The old alkie would have fled under a concerted attack, but in the end their patience was rewarded without any such unpleasantness. As two constables bundled their fellow citizen into a van, the gulls descended in a frenzy.

Bob was starving, though not that starving, and likewise penniless. The practical solution was to visit someone who might feed him. He looked at his watch. Bang in between meal times. Where would he go, anyway? Since he'd been away, he'd lost touch with people, at least not kept in touch to the extent that he could pony up and just say, "Hi, I'm hungry, feed me." Well, he could, but it would involve a loss of face that he wouldn't countenance, a whole story of flash fucker goes away to university, showed up the other day trying to cadge something to eat, fuckin waster. No, wasn't going to happen. Even his auntie and uncle would speak to his parents and a new narrative would be conceived which he had no desire to be a part of. Anonymity in this big village was what he craved right now.

Rising again, he went down Marischal Street to the harbour, and walked the length of the docks. Quiet as the grave on a grey

Sunday. He sat down at the end of Pocra Quay and resolved to stay there until a boat passed. Dark clouds blew up the river, but no shipping either coming or going. He abandoned his plan and strolled among the squat terraces and sheds of Footdee, hunched against the North Sea. The beach opened up before him. You could hear the wind. White horses broke an iron-dark sea, growing into breakers which thundered as they hit the shore. The stupid fucking beach. Bob was a connoisseur. In one of his fantasy lives he travelled the globe and wrote reviews. Sandy Bollocks, Beach Correspondent. There was a part of him that loved Aberdeen Beach. The romance was almost too much to bear. There had been a day when he had found himself, through no design, walking with Diane Dewar and her dog and they had just been messing about and chasing one another with seaweed and laughing and barking and they suddenly found themselves tripping over the dog and she fell onto him and time stood still in the sand and then there it was. First kiss. Just happened without thinking and every synapse went into overload at once. But it was still one stupid fucking beach. What was essentially a glorious two-three mile sweep of sand between the mouths of the two rivers was gashed every hundred yards by barnacled wooden groynes that stretched from the concrete slope up to the prom out into the water. They couldn't have built anything uglier. Except they had. Looming to the northwest, across the links, the ICI chemical works stood sticking two fingers up at the world, belching yellow smoke. Whatever shite they made in there-fertiliser, somebody had once told him-they had put all their efforts into making sure it produced the most evil stench known to man. It was like there must have been a war going on in Aberdeen Corporation between the tourist board and the planning department. Because, unaccountably, the old Granite City was a trippers' mecca of sorts. Every Glasgow Fair the denizens of the Dear Green Place who couldn't afford Blackpool pitched up in respectable numbers and laughed at hypothermia for a few days, and the Prom, Pavilion, Washington and Inversnecky Cafes enjoyed a brief bonanza during which they built up fat to get them through the harsh winter.

The darkening skies rolling in on a strengthening wind backing to the north had threatened it for a while and now horizontal rain began to whip into Bob's face. He quickened his pace, pulling his jacket round him as the rain turned to hail.

In a further insult to the natural splendour of the beach, concrete shelters had been erected every so often along the prom. He ran to the nearest one and wedged himself into the least windy corner. He was not alone.

A large police constable on the cold concrete bench that ran along the back of the shelter. He turned to the new arrival. "Fit the fuck you daein here?"

"I might ask you the same question."

"I'm the bobby, I ask the questions."

"I'm a Bobby too, ken."

"Smert cunt. Fit like onywey?"

"Fuckin' freezin." The officer looked quizzically at him. "I'm oot for a walk, a'right?"

The big copper sparked up a cig and sighed out a cloud. "Would you believe, 'is is my fuckin beat."

Bob sniggered. He jerked his head in the direction of the carney. "You been in ony high speed chases on 'e dodgems lately?"

The fat polis leapt remarkably nimbly to his feet and grasped his victim in a headlock. Bob grabbed a meaty thigh and managed to jerk it off the ground, collapsing them both onto the hard concrete. They wrestled unprofessionally, but it was an unequal struggle, and ended with the big man sitting on Bob McMillan's back, still puffing on his fag. He grabbed Bob's wrists and handcuffed him.

The crackle of the police radio interrupted the detainee's protests, "Control to 246. Control to 246. Over."

The cop, breathing hard after his unwonted exertion, fished out his radio and pressed the talk button. "246 to control. Fit seems tae be 'e problem? Over."

"You, a'right, 246? Over."

"Ay, fine. Jist puggled fae crime-fightin, ken. How can I be of assistance? Over."

"Bit ay a domestic. 35 Constitution Street."

"Christ, why is it aye Constitution Street? I can nivver spell it right. Could they nae ging roon 'e corner intae Park Street? Fit's happenin, onywey?"

"It seems a hamster's disappeared... You still there, 246? Over."

"I am. You're kiddin me, obviously."

"They think it's maybe gone under the floorboards. Wee loon's takkin a total heider, apparently."

"So fa taks 'e rap here. Is it the owners for criminal negligence or 'e hamster for abscondin?"

"I'll leave that to your discretion after you've gathered a' the evidence, 246. Look on 'e bright side. It'll get you oot this wither and you might get a cuppae tea and a biscuit if you play your cairds right. Out."

"If you could see me now you would notice that I was shakking ma heid, control. On ma wye. Oot."

Under his arse the constable could feel Bob McMillan convulsing with laughter. As he rose and replaced his radio the prisoner scrambled to his feet and legged it off down the prom.

"Here, come back wi' my cuffs, McMillan! STOP THAT MAN!"

As Bob ran, he was looking back at the fat constable as he too quickened his pace. "You'll never take me alive, stupid copper", were the last words he uttered before turning his face straight into the fist of the only public-spirited individual on the beach that day.

# 12

He came to. Hail bounced off him and a shivering small girl was shaking him with one hand. In the other she held a scabby rag doll. She wasn't exactly in rags herself, but her clothes were tired-looking, old-fashioned, kind of Oxfam. There was no sign of Police Constable 246 or his mystery assailant, and he was no longer wearing handcuffs.

She spoke. "You've got a jeely nose."

Bob touched his face and confirmed that there was blood on his fingers. "Fit happened?"

"You ran away from the policeman and he shouted, 'Stop that man' and then this other boy hit you and the bobby took your handcuffs off and then they both just walked away. Why did he let you go?"

"We were jist messin aboot. He's my mate's big brither. Where did you show up fae?"

"I saw it all. When I saw the policeman coming I went down on to the slope behind the fence there and waited till he went away again. I dinnae like going down there cos ay the wooden things."

Aye, they're ugly, eh?

"They're worse than that. They're evil. They'll bring you nothin but bad luck."

"Aye, OK. Tak it easy, Cassandra."

"My name's nae Sandra. But you can call me Sandra if you like. Can you get up? We should go back in the wee hoose. It's dry."

In the shelter Bob reassembled himself as best he could and tried to make sense of the situation. He looked at the little girl. She was really tiny, and pale. White as a sheet. "How old are you?" was the first question that came to mind.

"I'm eleven."

"You're nivver elivven!"

"I am. I'm just wee."

She held his gaze, and as he studied her face, her eyes looked as if they'd seen a good deal more than eleven years' worth.

They sat in silence as Bob pondered this latest development. He was confused, still a bit shaken up from the blow to the heid, he supposed. "Why would you hide from the polis? You some kind ay criminal mastermind?" he inquired.

No reaction.

"OK, you're nae gonnae answer that withoot a lawyer present. I can understand that. Alright. Let's try this one. What in the name ay Christ are you doing oot here by yersel in this wither?"

The wee lassie shrugged. "What about you, Bobby?"

"Ach, well. I'm...... Haud on, how do you ken my name?"

"I'm observant."

"What? Listen, this is a bit weird. In answer to your question, I dinnae hiv a clue fit I'm daein here either, but that disnae metter.

Fit's important is that we get you hame. Faraboot do you stay?"

She stared straight ahead.

Bob tried again. "Come awa', I'm trying tae help here. Your mummy and your daddy'll be worried sick about you." No answer, but silent tears welled up in her eyes and rolled down her cheeks. "Hey, I'm sorry, I didn't mean to upset you. Will you jist tell me what's the matter."

"Nothing, right. I'm just lonely today. Just like you, Bobby."

"I'm nae…"

"Aye, you are."

"Right. This is gettin us nowhere… You gonnae tell me your real name?"

"I can't."

"Jeez, you're nae makkin 'is very easy. If you dinnae tell me, I'm gonnae call you Uglina."

"Uglina!"

"Take it or leave it. OK, let's look at this situation logically. If we stay here we're both gonnae catch pneumonia. So we're gonnae go tae my flat. I've nae got nae money and I dinnae suppose you're an eccentric millionaire either, so we're gonnae have tae hoof it. It's a bit ay a hike, but I dinnae see ony alternative. You up for it?" She nodded. "Come on, let's go."

Night had fallen as they walked through the biting wind that cut across the Beach Boulevard in a silence broken by the chattering of the girl's teeth. Bob took off his jacket. "Here, pit this on."

"It's a bittie big for me, isn't it? And besides, you're freezin too."

"I'll be fine, I've got lots of layers. You can wear it like a coat. I insist."

She put it on. Bob laughed. "There you go. Damn stylish, if you ask me."

"I look stupit."

"Not at all. It's the wye fashion's gan, trust me."

She smiled. Down Market Street, across the bridge, and up Vicky Road, Bob's questions were met with tight-lipped silence and no eye contact. Eventually he gave up. As a police car passed she grabbed and hid behind him till it was gone. She looked up at Bob. "Please don't tell them about me. You've got to promise you won't phone them or anything."

"Listen, I'm nae a big fan ay the boys in blue masel, but in this case I'm sure they could help you…"

"No! If you dinnae promise I'm awa." Genuine fear and tears. "Here, have your stupit jacket back. I thought I could trust you."

"Whoa! OK! OK! I promise. I winna let anything bad happen to you. But what I dinnae get is why you're so sure you can trust me."

"If I cannae trust you, Bobby, who can I trust?"

"Dinnae worry, you can, but, Christ, this maks nae sense. Come on, we're nearly there."

In the flat Bob tidied up a bit, got the gas fire going and they sat

41

in front of it on the carpet for a good fifteen minutes before his brain had warmed up enough to formulate a plan. He carried it out, fishing about down the back of the armchair. Despite lacerations from upholstery pins, he continued doggedly. The first few coins he found were just coppers, then, just when he thought he was out of luck, there it was, larger and polygonal. He held it up in triumph. "The two-armed bandit pays out again!"

She smiled. "What are you going to buy with it?"

"Chips. I'll be back in no time."

"You cannae go out like that."

"Eh?"

"You've still got a bloody nose and now your hand's bleedin."

On the way to the chipper, Bob tried to make sense of it. The right thing to do was to get the wee lassie back to her mum and dad. That much was obvious. But it wasn't that simple. She wouldn't tell him anything. Why was she frightened of the cops? He knew that the right thing to do was to call the police, but he had promised not to. And for some reason that promise seemed really important. But the weirdest thing was that she seemed to kind of know him. He couldn't put his finger on it, but it felt like he couldn't lie to her. As things stood, what was clear was that he alone was responsible for her welfare, but Jesus, he could hardly look after himself, let alone a bairn. Well, he'd do his best, that's all he could do. For the moment she was warm, in a minute she'd have a wee bit scran inside her.

When he got back, she had fallen asleep in front of the fire. He sat down beside her and shook her gently. "Here we go. Hope you like salt and vinegar."

She sat up and they shared the poke of chips. He tried another question. "When did you last eat?"

"Long time ago."

"Well, stick in. Sorry there's not more."

"It's brilliant, Bobby. This is like *Little House on the Prairie*."

Bob grinned. "Ya think?"

"Do you want to say grace?"

"Na, you're OK. You?"

"God bless our chips, and make sure Bobby cheers up. Amen. This is my favourite meal ever."

"Think nithin o't. So, what are we going to do with you?... If you just tell me where you bide, I'll take you back right now, and then everything'll be alright, won't it?" Her face fell, and she looked up at him and shook her head. "Are you gonnae tell me what you're runnin away from?"

"I'm really sleepy now."

"Jeez! OK. Well. I'm obviously nae gonnae pit you oot in the rain, so you're stayin here. My mate's not back tonight, so you can sleep in the bedroom through there."

"Will Dave nae mind?"

"Na. Like I say, he's round at his ma's tonight, I think.... Whoa, haud on, how do you know about Dave?"

"I telt you, I'm observant."

43

"'Is is too mad."

She ate the last chip and yawned. "Can I go to bed now?

"Aye, I suppose. Lavvy's on your left, kitchen's efter that and then the bedroom's straight in front ay you. Help yersel tae anything that's nae nailed doon. You gonnae be warm enough?"

She nodded. "I'm fine now. You're a really good guy, Bobby. Dinnae let anybody tell you different."

"I'll tell them Uglina said so."

She smiled, picked up the doll, and left the room, closing the door behind her. Bob was tired himself, but mostly he was totally confused. As Sundays went, this had been one of the strange ones. He was apprehensive. What had he got himself into here? There was no way she could stay after tonight. He couldn't look after her. But where would she go? And here was the crazy bit. He had the weird impression that it was her that was looking after him. That made no sense at all. Maybe he was just losing it. She was real enough, though, she ate chips. Out in the lobby the bathroom door closed, and then Dave's bedroom door. He went and brushed his teeth, then undressed and lay down on his bed. He felt OK. The darkness had gone. He turned out the light and drifted off to sleep.

# 13

Aaaaaaaah! Ya fuckin bastard! She flew out of the unfamiliar shower, a scalded cat, danced across the lino and back, gingerly reached behind the curtain and turned the heat down. She ruled out the idea of a luxurious soak in the bath instead. Heather and Jean would be wanting in, and she couldn't be late, not today of all days. Definitely a big one. Exciting. Brand spanking uncharted waters! She grinned at herself in the mirror, the new girl at Vincent, Sprott, Provan and Kelty, Writers to the Signet, Queen Street, Edinburgh. It was like starring in her own movie. Rain battered the frosted window.

# 14

Bob awoke from a dream of Morag. Reality was less promising. The rent had to be paid. On the plus side, it was giro day. On the negative, the cheque wouldn't cover the rent arrears. The manny would certainly be round. Perhaps he was outside the door right now. Bob stuck his head into the bedroom. The kid had gone. Her doll, though, lay on the bed. He threw on some clothes and quickly vacated the premises.

A bitter boreal wind blew a strong stink of fish from the market in his face as he made his way down the hill into town. In the harbour, though, a lot of the fishing boats seemed to have been replaced by bigger ships bearing the logos of multinational corporations, in the same way as local accents in the bars and clubs seemed to have been supplanted to some degree by American and English ones since his return. The black scunner engulfed him once more. At the broo, he took his place and didn't even get annoyed at the snail's pace of the queue. It didn't matter. It wasn't like he had any plans.

Having cashed the cheque, he bought the *Press and Journal* and wandered aimlessly eastwards again. The people he passed seemed alien, unreal. He considered going in by to see his ma in Taylor's, but felt he might have to justify his existence in some way, and thought better of it. Past Marischal College and the police in Queen Street, he sat down on the steps of the Arts Centre, and wondered what the fuck to do with the rest of his day, his life. Faustus sprung to mind. By Bob's choice of studies, he too had effectively ruled out medicine, the law and the ministry. Was the infernal doctor of Wittenberg right? Was necromancy really the only viable option? Hunger was real enough, and led him into the Gordon Café. He ordered a black pudding roll and his first cup of tea, closed off the world around him and spread the paper out on the table.

Three slow cups later he felt himself more *au fait* with the minutiae of life in the North-East of Scotland than anybody really needed to be, and had made it through to the sports. To put off the inevitable end which was now in sight, he got himself another tea, and settled down to go through the racing. Picking winners with the care of someone who actually intended putting money on every race, he whiled away a further twenty minutes going through the cards at Kelso, Uttoxeter and Chepstow. In his high-rolling reverie, he betted cannily through the day, backing several successful favourites, picking out some longer-priced each-way shots in the handicaps. Now it came to the last race of the day, and he could afford to take an outrageous punt on a rank outsider. It was a cavalry charge, twenty-three runners. The connection he made with Rag Doll, number 16, was subconscious, but the horse fitted the bill. Absolutely no form, a plooky-faced apprentice claiming 7lbs. up, didn't even get a mention in the betting forecast, you'd have to be able to get 66–1, surely.

# 15

"Hi, honey, I'm home."

Dave Bruce entered the living room and collapsed in the armchair. Bob was lying on his bed. They remained in silence for a while. Dave eventually summoned up the energy to take his shoes and socks off. Finally Bob broke the ice.

"Fuckin shut it, eh."

"Dinnae. I'm nae in 'e humour." Dave inspected his feet, then stretched one out into Bob's face. "See 'at. 'At's a fuckin blister, min! I've fuckin walked 'e length ay Anderson Drive today, Woodside tae Holburn Street and then back up tae Mastrick. And how many hearin aids did you sell, David? Thank you for askin, Robert, I sold one poxy hearin aid, as it happens, went back up tae Ferret's, asked him if I could get my commission up front. It's only a fuckin tenner. Sleekit fucker went ootay the room tae get it. I wait for a bit, then I ging in and see his ma, and she tells me he's fucked aff oot and he winna be back for oors. I'm gonnae wring the scrawny wee cunt's neck, I swear I am. Christ, I dinnae get paid till the end of next month, either. How the fuck are we gonnae pye 'e rent?" He buried his face in his hands and silence fell again.

"I'm no chiropodist, Davie, but jist bide there a minute."

Bob returned with a basin of steaming water and two cups of tea. "Now stick your feet in 'at and hearken to the tale of my strange two days. The first thing you should know is that the rent has been paid."

"Eh? You actually manage tae tap some money aff Roddy?"

"Even stranger 'an 'at." And Bob related the story…

"… so I ging in aboot 'e bookie's, and right enough, he's got Rag Doll at 66–1, and I think, fuck it, easy come, easy go, and I stick a quid on 'e cuddy's nose and settle doon tae listen tae it disappear doon 'e Swanee. First few furlongs, disnae even get a mention. Eventually the boy goes 'And the back marker as they round the turn is Rag Doll, three lengths adrift of the field.' Well, I get up to go and I'm just at the door when the boy taks an eppy and I hear him gan 'Rag Doll, Rag Doll, Rag Doll' like a raj, and bugger me if she disnae come right through 'e field in 'e final furlong and tak it by a heid. I'm doon on the flair like a shot, and I find my ticket…"

"Sixty-six quid! Ya jammy hooer!"

"… and this is where it gets strange."

"I thought 'at business wi' the wee lassie was quite strange."

"OK. Check 'is. I stroll up tae 'e counter in a fairly self-satisfied manner, I've got tae say, and I hand ower my slip. Wifie jist stares at it for a bit, like she's glaikit. Efter a bit she gies me a soor look and gings ower tae 'e gaffer. I'm gettin a wee bittie impatient here, I'm wantin tae get my hands on 'e siller, like, cannae see fit 'e problem is. I look ower, and the fuckin bookie's got a face like a bulldog lickin pish aff a nettle. They disappear oot the back and eventually the wifie comes back wi' a big wad ay cash in baith hands. And she sits doon and she starts countin it oot… and then she keeps on countin it oot. Now, I dinnae hae a clue fit's gaun on here, I just wish she'd gie me my winnins so I can be on my wye. But she's still countin. Eventually she's done and she looks up at me wi' a big sigh and says, 'You'd better check it,' and pushes this dirty big pile ay used notes ower tae me. You would have been proud of me, David. I picked it up, stuck it in my inside pocket, said 'It's OK, you have an honest face,' and managed to leave the establishment at a cool saunter, though I was sure a'body in the shop could hear my heart thumpin. Louped on the bus, got back here, took 'e rent money round tae 'e manny, and I've been lyin here in a state of blissful incredulity ever since."

"Fuck! May I ask how much?"

"Six hundred and seventy pounds."

"How much?"

"You heard me right."

"Jesus! So they must have thought..."

"Obviously."

"It'll be 'at stupit roond full stop ye dae."

"I hadnae thought ay that. Could be, right enough. Artistic punctuation, min. It's underrated. Oh, I forgot. One more weird thing. As I was coming oot ay 'e bookie's. 'E wee lassie was there."

"Get away."

"Ay. Like she knew. I gid her a tenner, telt her I'd gie her the doll back. She says, 'No, look after it. I'll get it some day. I'm too old for dolls.' And she was aff."

"Ya jammy bastard. Fit you gonnae dae wi' 'e money?"

"We, David. What are *we* gonnae dae wi' it?"

"Na, it's your siller, man."

"Christ knows you've bailed me out enough times."

"Ay, but not on quite such a grand scale."

"Onywey, we should go somewhere."

"I agree. Hole?"

"As good a place to start as onywey."

A knock at the door. Dave, Lazarus with wet feet, rose and admitted a breathless Mrs. McMillan, with a neatly ironed and folded pile of washing. Bob had kind of noticed how thin she'd got over the weekend, but it hadn't really registered till now. "Fit like, David? 'Is lot's yours, eh? Ower big for Robert, right enough. Will I jist pit it in your bedroom?"

"Aye, thanks, Mrs. Mac. You didnae hae tae. Will I pit 'e kettle on?"

"Na, I'm grand, David. It's nae bother. Robert's obviously pit it in wi' his by mistake, like."

Dave returned to the comfort of the armchair and they waited. When Bob's mum re-entered, wild-eyed, she held the doll. "Far did you get 'is, David?"

"Nithin tae dae wi' Dave. Lang story, ma."

The fire was on, but she was shivering. "I've got a' night."

"I ran intae 'is wee lassie yesterday. It's hers."

"Fit wee lassie?"

"Dinnae ken her name."

"How aul' wis she?

"She wis elivven."

"Far did you meet her?"

"Met her at 'e beach. Fit's up, ma?"

In some distress, but almost inaudible. "Kirsty…"

"Fit ye on aboot, Mrs. McMillan?"

"I dinnae even ken, David. Fit were you gonnae dae wi' 'is?"

"Said I'd gie it back tae her one day, Ma."

"'Is maks nae sense. I'm gonnae hing ontae it, Robert."

"Ony special reason?"

"Cannae explain it now, son. Maybe if 'e quine wants it back some day she'll come and find me, afore it's ower late."

"Fit'll I tell her if she asks me far it is?"

"Tell her it was a' my fault, Bobby, and I'm sorry."

And she was gone. Through the window Bob watched her come out on the street and slump, distraught and weeping, against the car in the streetlight, clutching the doll to her like it was a real bairn.

Fifteen minutes later the lads found themselves in the 19th Hole at a table by the window overlooking the mouth of the Dee and the harbour lights, pints of heavy and toasties within their grasp.

"So, fit ye thinkin?" Dave enquired.

"Apart from a spot of wild speculation aboot ma ma's strange behaviour, Edinburgh."

"When?"

"'Is wikkend?"

"Aye. Why nae? I'll need tae get 'e car back on 'e road."

"We could train it."

"Na, I cannae leave it oot in Kintore forivver onywey. I'll get Gogs tae come oot and get it stairted. Friday mornin?"

"Will he nae be workin? Will you nae be workin?"

"Blood is thicker than water, Robert. He owes me one. And as far as Ferret and his stupit fuckin hearin aids is concerned, he can awa' and fuck himsel'. Far we gonnae stay?"

"I d'a ken. Somebody's flair."

"Somebody's flair? Hey, it's nae my money, Bob, but in Torry terms at least, you are more or less a millionaire. I'll book us a hotel, eh?"

"A hotel?"

"Aye."

"Aye. OK, then." Bob laughed. "Ken 'is, I've never stayed in a hotel. Except on holiday. 'Is is brilliant."

"Leave it tae me, pal." Dave Bruce drained his pint. "Another one here, or will we head intae town?"

"Prince ay Darkness?"

"Why ever not?"

The publican had come out from behind the bar and stood by their table. He looked over Bob's shoulder and spoke. "I cannae hae ye in here, sweetheart. I'll lose ma licence."

Bob turned and double-took. "Uglina! Fit you daein' here?"

"I never said thank you."

"Nae necessary, darlin."

"Aye it is. And thank you, Dave, for letting me stay."

"How did ye ken far tae find us?"

"And fit wye div ye ken ma name?"

"I'm observant. I telt you." And she was gone.

As Dave and Bob started their descent of the steps at the side of St. Nicholas Kirkyard, they heard an altercation from below in the darkness of Correction Wynd.

A man's voice: "Fuck you, ya fuckin hooer!"

A woman's: "Fa you cryin a hooer, ya fuckin ignorant airse. I spik tae fa'ivver I wint tae spik til, right. I go farivver I wint tae go."

The man: "Ay, that'll be right. Just tell me fit ye were daein' in his hoose."

The woman: "I've telt ye! He's Karen's brither, she's ma best mate, they both live there. Fit d'ye want me tae say?"

"I'm nae daft, fuck's sake! Just admit you were fuckin shaggin him"

"I wish I hid. It'd be mair fun than this shite."

As Dave and Bob arrived at the bottom of the steps they both heard and witnessed, in the shadows at the end of St. Nicholas Lane, a blow that sent Kim Anderson sprawling on the cobbles. Igor the Biker stood over her. Once again, Bob McMillan was surprised by the rogue Bruce gene. With the speed of a mutant whippet, Dave had nashed across the street. The force of his collision with Igor sent the big biker crashing into the wall behind him. It was over in a second. Igor swung a wild, enraged haymaker that brushed Dave's temple. Off-balance, he was wide open to a swift one-two that left him slumped, spark-out, at the foot of the wall.

Bob stood aghast at Dave Bruce's side. "Shite, man, I fear you have just made a powerful enemy. Nice shots, by the way!"

Dave turned to Kim. "You OK?"

She nodded tearfully. "I'm fine. Stupit fuckin bastard!"

"Do you want a help up?"

"Leave me alane! Get your hands aff me!"

"OK. OK. Take it easy. I'm just saying, probably best to shoot the craw before…. Ken."

Bob helped out. "You can come for a drink with us if you want. We're just going in the Prince there."

"FUCK OFF, BOBBY!"

"I just thought you could maybe dae wi' a drink, like...."

"FUCK OFF, BAITH AY YIZ!" And she scrambled to her feet like a new-born foal and weaved off towards Markies. Igor the Biker was not yet back on script and there seemed nothing to hang about for. The lads walked the few steps to the doors of the Prince of Wales and pushed them open.

The next morning, she wrapped up as warm as she could, checked the tenner in her pocket, and started walking with only the roughest idea of what direction she should take. It hosed it down with rain all day, but she pressed on. That evening, at a filling station outside Stonie, she bought Hula Hoops and a Jolly Jelly and her enquiries confirmed she was going the right way, and that she would not reach her destination on foot by the weekend. A kind lady, a zookeeper as it turned out, overheard the conversation, told Uglina they shared a journey's end and invited the wee drowned rat to jump in. Throughout the drive the wee girl gave characteristically little away apart from revealing that her name was Lori Beth, but managed to extract many tales of adventures in the menagerie trade from her chauffeur. It sounded almost as much fun as being a detective. What was established before she fell asleep was that young Alison had no idea where she was staying that evening, and so it came to pass that the next few nights were spent on the zookeeper's sofa, and the days making free with her kitchen and her Yellow Pages and phone.

# 16

Friday morning found Bob and Dave at the bus station, at the open door of the country bus to Huntly. The driver leaned out. "I cannae wait ony longer, ma bonny loons. Are ye gettin on or are ye nae?"

Gogs piled round the corner, bearing a large toolbox and a can of petrol.

Dave berated him. "Fuck's sake, Gogs. You're disrupting the hale transport infrastructure ay the Garioch here. Loup on, min."

He did so. "I'm nae late, I'm almost early. I hid tae ging in tae work tae chore 'is lot and then I hid tae pretend I'd got diarrhoea. Took a while. Nivver mind. We're here noo. Dinnae spare the horses, driver. Get yer kicks on 'e A96!"

A holiday spirit reigned as they rolled out down George Street and through Woodside and Bucksburn into the countryside beyond the airport. Dave Bruce had packed two bags, one piece of normal luggage for the trip and one of equal size devoted to snacks. As the team breakfasted on rowies, Irn Bru, crisps and Mars Bars the bus pulled up the Tyrebagger past the autumn colours of Kirkhill Forest and through Kinellar. It was still cold but the sun shone unseasonably.

"How's the hearin aid, business, Dave?" Gogs asked, grinning over at Bob.

"Fit?"

"I was sayin, 'How's it gaun wi' the hearin aids?'

"Sorry?"

"Have – you – sold – many – hearin – aids?"

"I'm still nae gettin it, Gogs. Fit ye sayin?"

And Kintore hove into view. They piled out and struggled to the outskirts of town. At the gate to a field Dave put his bags down and the others followed suit.

Gogs sat down on the toolbox. "Christ, Davie, is it much further, min? 'Is box isnae light, ken."

"Well, 'e thing is, it *shouldnae* be much further. In fact, it should be right here."

"Fit?"

"Unless I've went mental, 'is is far I left it."

"Na, shite, min, you've made a mistake."

"Dinnae think so. I recognise the fairmhoose up there. I even recognise the coos. 'Is is too mad."

"Maybe somebody's chored it."

"Na, I ken 'at motor like 'e back ay my hand, and even I couldnae get it stairtit. I'm pretty sure it didnae hiv nae petrol left in it onywey, like."

A tractor was coming up the road, holding up a long line of traffic.

Bob went and sat on the gate. "Well, I'd say we are, as we doctors like to put it, totally fucked. Only thing we can dae is get 'e bus back into Aiberdeen and tak 'e train."

"Wait a minute," Dave protested. "I'm a Ford Escort doon on 'e deal here."

The tractor turned off the road to face the gate and a turkey-necked old teuchter jumped down in some agitation. "Get doon aff 'at fuckin gate!" he yelled, wild-eyed.

Bob eyed the old man quizzically but evidently did not comply with his request speedily enough. The ancient agriculturalist scuttled forward like a spider, grabbed Bob's ankle and heaved him off his perch splashing into the huge coo-shitey puddle at the foot of the gate. Returning to the tractor he emerged with a spade, smacked Bob with it and then began spinning dervish-like in anticipation of retaliation. "I'm nae feart o' you young anes. I'll tak yiz a' on," he quavered.

An absolute impasse had developed. If any of the lads advanced on their adversary, they risked a heavy, sharp-looking spade in the coupon. If the old nutter concentrated his attack on one of them, then the others would certainly take him out. And so he kept on whirling. After a minute they had relaxed slightly. After two minutes their apprehension had turned to fascination and some degree of admiration at the aged son of the soil's stamina. Around the three-minute mark the spade flew off raggedly into a ditch behind Gogs, narrowly missing him, and the old guy went down like a sack of shite. Bob McMillan advanced on him and aimed a kick into his midriff. Dave and Gogs were on him like a shot and held him back.

"Leave it, Bobby, fuck's sake!" Dave Bruce spun Bob round and pushed him away. He dropped to his knees beside the farm labourer. "C'm'ere, Gogs. I'm nae sure 'is is cool. Can you hear me? Are you OK, min?"

The old man stirred slightly. His voice was barely audible. "I feel affa dizzy."

"'At goes wi'oot sayin," Dave reassured him. "Anythin else?"

The old man began to sing weakly.

"Oh, beat the drum slowly and play the fife lowly,

And play the deid march as you carry me alang;

Tak me tae the green valley, there lay the sod ower me,

For I'm a young cowboy and I ken I've done wrang."

And his eyes closed. Gogs shook him. "C'moan, min. Stay wi' me. Bobby, get up tae 'at fairmhoose and ca' an ambulance. I think we're losin him."

"Serves him right."

"BOBBY!"

"Ay, OK, OK. I'm gan."

The farmer's wife was inured to the sight of men covered in shite, but as she opened the door to the panting stranger, she was nonetheless surprised. "Fit d'ye wint?"

"Am...bul...ance.... Auld guy.... Doon by the road.... Think... he might... be deid."

She made the call, threw on a coat, and they hurried out, pursued by two barking collies. As they rounded the corner of the house and looked across the field history was repeating itself. Down by the gate the old man once again spun his spade vigorously as

Dave and Gogs looked on in astonishment. "Fa's the ambulance for?" she asked.

"Boy wi' the shovel."

"Disnae look very deid tae me."

She ran down the field through the scattering cattle. Shouting at the top of her voice. "Jockie! Pit 'at spade doon, ye feel gype!"

The old man's spinning became less regular as he registered the farmer's wife's approach, and ground to a halt as the gate stopped her progress. "Fit div you think you're daein', ye daft aul' goat?"

He reeled erratically as he approached the gate, pointing wildly about him. "They're rustlers, Mrs. Davidson!"

"Oh, for the love o' Christ, Jockie, they're nae rustlers. Awa up tae the hoose and I'll mak you some denner."

Looking sheepish, he stumbled forward, slipping into the shitey puddle before slithering over the gate and making his way unsteadily up the field.

Mrs. Davidson surveyed the lads. "Sorry, boys, Jockie gets a wee bittie over-excited sometimes, but he's hairmless really."

"You could have fooled me."

"Fit are you daein here, onywey?"

"We're lookin for a car."

"Wis that 'e car 'at wis parked right across 'is gate so we couldnae get 'e tractor in?"

Dave took responsibility. "Ay, I'm sorry, I broke doon, had to get it aff 'e road."

"You might hae telt us."

"Aye, I'm sorry, I didnae think… Could you tell us where it is now if you dinnae mind?"

"It's at Sandy Michie's gairage in Kintore there. It wis in an affa state, 'at motor. Fit a job he hid gettin it stairtit. He'd to get pairts oot fae Aiberdeen an' a'thing. Fit wye did you nae come lookin for it till now?"

"Didnae really have enough money."

"Well, awa and get your car. I'll gie him a phone and tell him you're comin."

"Thanks."

"Ay. Thanks for savin us."

"Think nothing o't. Sorry aboot Jockie. He thinks he's John Wayne. But we've got tae look efter them a', haven't we?"

"Aye. Well, bye then."

"Bye, bye. Drive carefully, boys."

As Bob, Dave and Gogs made their way through the autumn sunshine down the A96 back into Kintore the ambulance sped by them, siren blaring.

Sandy Michie was a large man, in his sixties and a boiler suit, with two tufts of unkempt white hair fringing the runway in the middle of his head and a red face, sitting at a desk in a wee office at the back of his establishment. Dave stepped in, followed by the others. Michie looked up at them over the top of his specs. "'At's some motor you've got there. Which one of you clowns is the owner?"

Dave raised his hand. The garage man shook his head. "Braks ma hert. Right, I've basically rewired it. Dinnae ken if ye were contemplatin suicide, but just in case you werenae, I've replaced your shocks and a' the brakes, discs and pads, and I've fixed your fuel leak. You ken you were awa to set yersel on fire there, don't you? 'At's if the faulty brakes didnae kill you first. Oot o' ma sight."

Dave hesitated. "Far's 'e car?"

"How many Ford Escorts d'ye see?"

Dave looked around, and sure enough, there was a sky-blue motor roughly matching the description over in a corner. Except he didn't recognise it. "That's nivver my motor."

"Ay, amazin, is it? They look better fan you clean 'em. You should try it some day."

"That's incredible! But how much do we owe you?"

"Well, I nivver mind getting pyed twice, but Doris Davidson's takkin' care o't. She said it was fine as lang as you didnae press chairges. Nae idea fit the feel aul bat's on aboot. Kent her for sixty year and I'm still nane the wiser."

Michie dismissed Dave Bruce's thanks, assured him that though, like everyone in the world of agriculture, Mrs. Davidson would not hesitate to tell you how hard times were, she had not yet contemplated selling her brand-new top of the range Jag, and requested that they never darken his doors again. For the first time the Escort started first time. They dropped Gogs off in Mastrick, swept down Anderson Drive, across the old bridge, up the hill past the city limits and they were on the open road. They enjoyed the novelty of the radio, blaring for the first time also in Dave's experience. As they pulled out of Stonehaven, he turned it down and spoke. "So, tonight, fit's 'e plan?"

"Café Royal for a start."

"Sounds flash. They gonnae let you in?"

"Cheeky cunt."

"You're still covered in shite, like."

"I might get changed, right enough, but it's jist a boozer, only mair picturesque, ken. I've managed tae track doon a couplae mates, so they should be along and then we'll see how we go. I just fancy a real good night on the lash, personally. Sound OK?"

"Admirable."

Dave turned the radio up again. Lena Martell sang "One Day at a Time", and the lads joined in lustily. They drove on until a huge sign announced "YE MAY GANG FAUR AND FARE WAUR". Hunger drove the car into the transport caff at Stracathro.

# 17

On his debut in the capital, Dave Bruce parked down Leith Walk, and as they strolled up Elm Row towards Princes Street Bob McMillan took on the role of tour guide, sharing memories of games at Easter Road, gigs at the Playhouse and gorgonzola and gavi at Valvona and Crolla. The North British Hotel loomed before them in all its opulence.

"Where's wir hotel?" inquired Bob. Dave gestured grandly. Bob looked doubtful. "Are you sure? Will they even let us in?"

"Indeed they will. We have a bookin and a wad ay cash. I'll dae the talkin."

The doorman, a veteran of the Second Boer War by all appearances, was obviously dubious too, but he opened the door for them. At reception a vision of loveliness in Dress Stewart was serving. Except she wasn't. She was ignoring them. There could be no mistaking the ignorance. Dave Bruce cleared his throat. She looked at him as if he hadn't flushed away properly.

"Can I help you?"

"In so… many… ways… But to business. I believe we have a reservation. I am Bruce and he is McMillan. And you are… Moira. How charming."

# 18

Showered, shaved and changed, Bruce and McMillan propped up the bar of the Café Royal. Conversation dwindled. Bob turned the discussion to music, always a safe bet in these circumstances.

"How do you rate 'e Squibs' new singer, by the way?"

"'E rid-heided loon? Mair than adequate, I thought. A regular visitor tae 'e Jimmy Shand Surplus Shop by all appearances."

"A fuckin riot ay tartan, certainly. Talkin ay claes, yon kiddies in 'e corner, bit ay a stab at a Coventry look, wid ye say?"

"Aye, smert, eh? 'At'll mak it up tae Aiberdeen in a couplay years."

They went back to their pints, taciturn but content. Dave Bruce was fine just drinking in the lofty, ornate, lavishly tiled, plastered and stained-glassed Victorian splendour. Nothing like this back in Ab! Bob wanted to make things happen, but had no idea how.

He tried again. "The thing is, normally, by the time you've got enough money tae enjoy yersel, you're too old tae dae it. Would you believe my da telt me that?"

"It dis seem oot ay character. Wouldnae hiv said flashes ay non-Calvinist insight were really his thing."

"You're nivver sure, eh?"

"Wis he pished at the time?"

"Aye."

Dave heaved a sigh of contentment. "Well, isn't this grand, Robert."

"It certainly is, David."

"The chink of glasses, happy, stylish people gathering for a night out, and here we are, a couple of high rollers just hit town ready to sample the best our capital has to offer in the way of carousal, strong drink and bonny lasses... oooh... check *her* oot, Bob."

"Eh?"

"Rid hair, jist come through the door."

"Oh Jesus... Oh Christ... Oh my God...."

"Get a grip, min... Fit's up wi' ye?"

"It's her."

"Fa?"

"Fa d'ye think?"

"Awa' you go.... Fit wid a good-lookin quine like 'at be daein gan aroon wi' a wee Lord ay the Rings runt like you... onywey, you said she wis in Frunce..."

"I thought she wis..."

"Well, naebody can accuse the last few days ay nae bein action-packed. Introduce me then..."

"Haud on a minute there! 'Is is a big moment for me. I've got tae think ay somethin tae say."

"Think quick, Bob. Here she comes…"

Morag McPherson approached, smiling less enigmatically than Mona Lisa, but certainly not grinning ear to ear. Bob knew that look well. Left him helpless every time. His legs turned to porridge and his bowels to water. Her advance was unhurried and even, and was stopped by Bob McMillan, who staggered back as she wrapped her arms round his neck and gave him a kiss that stopped conversations. As she released him, he struggled to put his spine back where it should be, stuck out an elbow, supported himself against the bar, and spoke.

"Pint ay heavy, is it, Morag?"

"God, I haven't had that in ages. Aye, alright, why not."

Bob put the order in. Dave coughed.

"Oh, you've never met Dave, have you?"

"Heard all about you, though."

Dave looked quizzically at Bob. "It's a' lies."

"You're not as fat as he said you were, right enough."

"Thanks, pal."

"I was expecting a hippopotamus or something…"

Bob intervened. "Aye, very good, Morag. Anyway, how've you been?…"

She shrugged. "I've got a job, though."

"Oh aye. Where?"

"Vincent, Sprott, Provan and Kelty."

"Wait a minute. You're kiddin me!"

"No. For real. I knew you would get it. Half the people in the office don't even get it, but I knew you would, if I ever saw you again."

"Where you livin?"

"Got a flat in the New Town."

"Flash bitch! How'd you manage that?"

"Sharing with lassies I knew at Uni. They'd a spare room. It's no ideal."

"Sounds pretty damn good tae me."

"Ach, we dinnae really get on. They were like Christian Union and all that."

"Whereas you were in league with Satan in a casual way."

"It is a brilliant flat though, Bobby. I'm trying to keep my nose clean these days."

"Come on. Name names."

"Heather Abernethy?"

Bob recoiled. "Oh no! What, with the bad breath and the plooks and the five o'clock shadow?"

"Not very gallant, but yeah."

"This is more serious than I thought. In the Hitler youth too, if I'm not mistaken."

"She was in the Conservative Students thing, aye."

"Right! A collaborator, like I said. Nothing as despicable as a Scottish Tory. I bet she supports Rangers, too…"

"… and Jean MacFadzean."

"Christ! She's a freemason, isn't she? How's the new job, at Vincent…?"

"…Sprott, Provan and Kelty of Queen Street. Bunch of arseholes, Bobby."

"You're very disloyal."

"Ach well, alright in their own way, I suppose. For lawyers. Just boring, like. No much talent, really."

"Well, that's a shame for you."

There was a silence during which Bob and Morag communicated perfectly adequately.

"Ditched him, by the way, Rabbie. Or he ditched me. Mr. X. Somewhere on the Riviera… Sorry if I hurt you… Listen, I've got to go. We're off to the flicks."

"Who's we?"

"Me and Simon." A big, sporty-looking lad smiled back at Morag from across the bar. "A colleague."

"Come on, Morag, we've got a lot of catchin up to do…"

The barman butted in. "40p."

"……. and here's your drink……."

"Have it on me."

"'Have it on me?' I'm fuckin buyin it."

"Have it on yourself, then. I'm sure you'll manage."

"Listen, I've got a lot tae tell you. A lot ay things have happened."

"I'll see you around, alright."

And she was gone, pausing only to collect Fucking Merchant Company Rugby Gorilla Simon, as he had recently been christened.

Dave Bruce spoke. "A little something tae chase it doon, Robert?"

"A large one." And he slumped, chin in hands, on the bar, his air that of a man who has just been hit with a sockful of shite.

Dave paid the barman and ordered more drinks. Another strawberry blonde entered the bar. This one was male, Dundonian and shifty-looking. He grinned when he clocked Bob and sidled over. "Fit like, Bobby loon?"

"Pure teckle an' aw that, Norrin. What you hehin'?"

"Eh'll just heh the usual."

"Fehf tehs and fehf pehs?"

"Demij, man!"

Dave Bruce leaned over. "Onybody gonnae spik English?"

"Dave Bruce, I have the honour to introduce Norrin Radd. Norrin Radd, Dave Bruce."

Dave looked perplexed. "The Silver Surfer?"

"The very man."

"You're nae how I pictured you."

"You're no how eh pictured you, ehther. You're no as fat as heh said you were."

"Fuck's sake, Bobby."

Bob moved the conversation on. "'E thing is, he's cried Bobby 'n'a, so the Silver Surfer avoids confusion."

Dave still looked perplexed. "Nae for me, it disnae. You're fae Dundee, if I'm nae mistaken. Correct me if I'm wrang, but the Silver Surfer's fae the planet Zenn-La."

"Reht on both counts. Eh'm impressed. Eh ehm a surfer though."

"Na. I'm nae haein 'at. Ye cannae hae Dundonian surfers."

"Och aye. It's gettin bigger every day."

"Fae Carnoustie tae the shores ay Lochee."

"Precehseleh."

"An' fit div you surfers drink?"

"Snehkbeht, mostleh."

As Dave attracted the barmaid's attention, the doors swung open again to reveal gypsies. A long-haired swarthy youth, festooned with jewellery and tattoos, in a long black leather coat of the style often worn by men simply referred to as the accused and a bandana, and a small, sexy-looking bottle blonde in a tracksuit top, a long sparkly green pencil skirt slashed all the way up the thigh and industrial strength make-up. There was something about them that made you instinctively check you still had your wallet. The boy's voice rang across the bar. "Check it oot, hen! A fat cunt wi' two Boabies!" He grabbed her hand and pulled her over to join the others.

The Silver Surfer turned to his companions. "Oh. Shite. Look out."

The loud new arrival grabbed both Bobbies in a headlock and banged their heads together. "We're speedin aff wir tits!" he announced. Releasing them, he grabbed Dave in a bone-crunching handshake. "How's it gaun, big man? Dave Bruce, I presume. C'm'ere, you're no so fat as he said you were, so you're no."

Bob sighed. "Dave, this is the Waltzer Monkey, and......."

The gypsy lad put an arm round his wee pal. "The Little Mermaid. Made her acquaintance oan the bus fae Glesca. Sooked us aff in the back seat."

The girl punched his arm viciously. "Shut it, you!"

73

"Only messin, doll. Or am I?"

Dave caught Bob's eye with a 'What the fuck?' look, before enquiring, "Dis onybody hiv real names aroond here?"

"Ay, ah'm Johnny Barr. He jist cries me the Waltzer Monkey cos I used tae work on the shows."

"And ah'm Kelly Reid. And ah've got nae idea why he caws me the Little Mermaid."

The Waltzer Monkey turned to Bob. "Here, you did English. Whit's that word for stranded on a desert island? No shipwrecked."

"Marooned?"

"Stoatin! Pint ay Tennent's for me, and whatever the young lady's havin."

"Rum and pep."

The Monkey held out his hand to Dave once more. He looked at him questioningly, but accepted it, and came away with a bag of powder. "Knock yersel oot and pass it on, man."

The Waltzer Monkey, true to form, took on the role of social secretary. He was very good at it, to be fair. Just made daft shite happen, effortlessly. Like a shark with blood, he could sniff a party out at a distance of several nautical miles. He was also, unaccountably, catnip to the lassies. A night out with the Monkey guaranteed an increase in your circle of female acquaintances.

As they finished their drinks he assumed control. "Right, we're awaw doon the Vinnie after this yin."

"Whit's the Vinnie?", asked the Little Mermaid.

"The St. Vincent Bar", explained the Silver Surfer. "It's a good shout. You'll love it."

"I like it here."

For a young man who prided himself in generating anarchy all around him, the Waltzer Monkey lived his life according to some strict precepts. "First rule ay a night oot, doll. Keep movin. You can always come back, but if you dinnae go, you dinnae know."

And so they found themselves on their way down Howe Street towards Stockbridge, speeding like nervous whippets. As the other lads arsed about, play-fighting and shouting, through grinding teeth and with pupils the size of 10ps the Surfer attempted to act on his new-found and urgent physical attraction to the Mermaid. "So whehr about in Glasgow are you from?"

"Ah'm no fae Glesca, ah'm fae Livvy."

"Livingston-largest town in West Lothian. Designated as such in 1962, it's the fourth post-war new town to be built in Scotland. Approximately 15 miles from Edinburgh and 30 miles from Glasgow. The River Almond flows through the town centre. It would be about the tenth biggest urban settlement in Scotland, am eh right? The area was historically dominated by oil shale mining. The new town designation attracted new light industries to the area, notably high technology and pharmaceutical."

"Whit?"

"Sorreh, eh studied geographeh at universiteh. What were you dehin in Glasgow?"

"Shoppin, but there's that many store detectives these days, all ah got was some bras and panties and stockins and suspenders and that, so ah decided tae heid hame, and then ah met Johnny at the bus station, and we decided tae come here instead."

"Well, eh'm glad you did."

"Why?"

"Em, eh dinneh ken. Are *you* glad you kehm?"

"Ken this, you're quite nosy. But aye, ah'm havin an OK time so far. Why do they caw you the Silver Surfer?"

"Cos eh'm a surfer."

"You're no silver, though."

"Na, the real Silver Surfer's an ehlien."

"Oh, right. Whit's he like? Ah bet he's a guid laugh and awbody likes him, like Mork, eh?"

"No, they dinneh lehk him at all most eh the tehm, and he's a bitteh miserable. This is what he says: 'Eh feel lehk, ken, in all the world there is no plehce for me, lehk. Exehled hehr upon the planet Earth eh am kindeh a strehnger among strehngers, an ehlien amongst the rehce eh men, ken'."

The Mermaid pointed up at the sky. "Jesus, did you see that wan?"

"What?"

"The UFO. That wis brilliant."

"Whehr?"

"It's gone noo, but it'll be back. You jist hae tae keep watchin."

"You're kiddin me on."

"No."

"You seen them before, then?"

"Oh aye, aw the time. Keep watchin."

"What am eh lookin for?"

"It changes. That wan there wis quite far away, but it wis really bright."

"Was it no a shootin star or somethin?"

"Naw. It moves aw ower the place."

"You rehlly belehve in all that shite?"

"Aye. Ah wis abducted by aliens wance. At least ah think ah wis, but ah might have imagined it, cos ah'd a teacher that said ah'd a fertile imagination."

"Whehr was this?"

"Livingston. Ah used tae see them aw the time, like."

"What?"

"Aliens. In Livvy."

"Why would ehliens come teh Livingston?"

"Cos it's a new toon, like. You can get money fae the cooncil if you want tae build factories an' that. They never actually telt me that was why, though, in fact they never said fuck all."

"Probableh couldneh spehk English."

"Ah never thought ay that, cos they aye can on the TV, but that'll be it right enough. Ah jist thought they were rude."

"What were theh lehk?

"Silver. Like the Surfer, eh? Aye, no completely, but mostly silver. But as time went by they got tae look mair like you and me."

"Did nehbody else seh them?"

"I dinnae think so, and that was the weird thing, cos ah thought they really stood oot."

"What happened when theh abducted you?"

"Well, it was wan night they'd parked their thing doon the end ay wir road…"

"Haud the bus! Theh'd a thing as well? What was that lehk?"

"Silver, and ah wis drawn intae it by a mysterious force."

"What wis it like insehd? What were they dehin, like?"

"It wis crap. It wis really clarty, didnae look like it had been cleaned for months, and they were jist sittin aboot, watchin TV and that. So ah started giein it a bit ay a tidy up, but they were dead ignorant like, wouldnae even move their feet, so ah thought, fuck you then, ah mean ah'm fucked if ah'm skivvyin for thae bastards if ah'm no even gonnae get a fuckin thank you for it, but ah couldnae leave cos there was nae doors or windaes or that so ah jist sat aboot for a bit and then they like took us for a bit ay a hurl and the boy was a shite driver cos he kept bumpin intae things. Ah mean it wisnae really his fault cos like ah say there wis nae windaes or fuck all so he couldnae see where he was gaun. Anyway, him and his mates jist had a laugh aboot it, didnae gie a fuck like, although some ay the others were lookin pissed aff but they kept their mooths shut. Ah think they were feart ay the boy cos he was a bittie raj. Drapped us aff in the toon, eventually, nae 'see ya laters,' nothin. Ah wis glad tae see the back ay them tae tell you the truth. Ah mean ah had an OK time, but we didnae get on, ken whit ah mean? You think ah'm mental, eh? Well ah'm no, right. There's fuck all wrang wi' me. Ah jist want them tae leave me alane."

"Who? The ehliens?"

"Aye. The aliens, the polis, you, fuckin all ay yiz."

At which point the Waltzer Monkey arrived at speed and scooped the Little Mermaid up in a fireman's lift. "C'moan tae, we're wastin VDT here. Ah'll pure race yiz aw!" And they were off down the hill in a ragged charge which ended in a breathless pile-up by the railings outside the St. Vincent Bar. Once again, he took charge. "Right, ah'll get them in. Norrin, awaw roon the corner and see who's oan at Tiffany's the night. Snakebite, aye?"

"No, eh'll heh a black velvet. Sweet stout, no Guinness."

The Vinnie was stappit and noisy, hoaching with some familiar faces and loads of new ones. Some of them were in fancy dress. Black and white was obviously the theme. They piled into the scrum at the bar and as the Monkey got the order in the Silver Surfer returned. "D'ye want the good news or the bad news?"

"Bad news every time."

"Reht, they're sold oot."

"Fa's sold oot?"

"Two Tone tour, man. Specials n'at. Ken? 'Gangsters'. Eh fuckin love that number. Eh wis rehdin aboot it in the NMEh. It's meant teh be some show."

The Mermaid was an optimist. "Whit's the good news?"

"There is no good news."

The Monkey's eyes narrowed. "You know whit there's no such thing as? Santy Claus. You know whit else there's no such thing as? A sold-oot show. Gie's a fiver each."

The Aberdonians protested.

"A fiver! Nae feart, are you, min?"

"It's nae the fuckin Rollin Stones!"

"'M'oan tae fuck, ya tightersed sheepshaggin cunts. Ah've got a good feelin about this. Could be the loveliest night ay the year, so it could!"

The Monkey paid for the drinks from the money he prised out of them, downed his lager in a oner, belched long and hard and made for the exit. "Behave yersels while I'm oot, kids, eh?" and he was off.

Dave took a shaky slug of his pint. "Dinnae ken aboot you, boys and girls, but I am buzzin like a jar full ay wasps."

"Hope teh fuck he gets theh tickets, man. Eh'm readeh teh dance ma ehrse aff."

"I'd pay good money to see that alone."

"How dae youse aw ken each ither?"

"We met at a gay leather bar in San Francisco."

"Whit were you daein in San Francisco?"

"Dinnae listen tae Dave, he's full ay shite. It wis a gay leather bar in Stornoway."

The Little Mermaid looked confused. The Surfer came to the rescue. "Me and Bobbeh and the Monkeh wis at universiteh hehr together. Geographeh, and English, and what did Johnneh deh?"

"Chemistry. Christ, min, you shared a flat wi' him. Did it nivver come up in conversation?"

"You know what, it never did." The Surfer pulled off his jumper, revealing a Dundee United shirt. "Fuck meh, eh'm perspehrin like a fuckin rehpist."

"And me and Robert here are mates fae school in Aiberdeen."

"And whit d'you dae noo?"

Bob fielded the question. "In my case, I dinnae dae sweet jack shite, David appears tae have become a hearin aid salesman, but I cannae see that lastin, and I've nae idea how Norrin here fills the unforgiving minute these days."

"Eh'm workin towards a professional surfin career."

"Yer airse. That's anither thing there's nae such thing as."

"There fuckin is. In California and Haweheh and that. And mehbe Peru."

"Na, I'm nae haein' that. Fit wye wid somebody pye you for jist surfin aboot?"

"You get sponsored for advertehsin shite when you're oot surfin. Ken, lehk Formula One?"

"Aye, stroll on! You're only wearin a pair ay swimmin trunks, aye? And you're wye oot at sea in the middle ay dirty big waves. Fit wye's onybody gonnae be able tae read fit's on yer skids? And even if somebody wis mental enough tae dae 'at, fit wye you plannin tae get oot tae California and Hawaii and Peru?"

"Eh've been working tae rehse the cash."

Bob shook his head and as the decibel level in the bar built, he drifted off into a conversation with Dave, but the Little Mermaid was intrigued. "So you *have* got a job."

"Well, no right noo, but eh had. Whit about you?"

"Snap. No right noo, but ah had a job too."

"What did you deh?"

"No. You first"

"Aye, OK. Reht. Well, lehk Dehvid thehr, eh used teh be a sehlsman."

"And whit did you sell?"

"Encehclopehdias. Door teh door. It wis murder."

"Crazy. Did you sell lots?

"Well, that depends how you look at it. Eh mehn, every tehm you sold a set you sold a lot eh books, but you could only sell them in sets."

"Uh-huh."

"And the deal was you didneh get eneh moneh unless you sold, so, you were under a bit eh pressure, lehk, if you were inteh ehtin and that kindeh stuff. You'd get drapped aff at these poxy schemes, and there'd be a tehm eh you, and between you you'd go round every fuckin gaff in the nehbourhood and treh and punt thehse books at them."

"How many did you sell?"

"None at all. Eh hed teh stop in the end cos eh wis suffering feh vitamin deficienceh and eh couldneh afford teh get meh suit dreh clehned and efter you've been oot in the rehn a few tehms you look like shite and folk winneh let you in enehweh."

"Hoo did you get intae their hooses in the first place?"

"It wis surprehsingly ehsy. Eh'll treh it on you."

"OK."

"Here goes. Ding dong."

"Aye."

"Hello, eh'm talkin teh everyone in the ehreha this evening."

"You're no fuckin talkin tae me, pal."

"Aye, well, it didneh work wi' everehbodeh."

"Just as well you never came roond oor hoose. If ma wee brither hadnae got you the dug wid've."

"Your turn."

"Well, ah never thought ah'd much prospects cos ah didnae want tae dae anythin, but, as it turned oot, ah did get a job."

"What did you deh?"

"Ah wis a shop assistant. Ah thought it would be rotten, but it was a laugh. We jist used to take the pish ootay the customers the hale time."

"What sort eh shop wis it?

"It wis an electrical shop, so it wis braw, cos you could watch the TV and listen tae music and ah wis seein the van driver, so we were shaggin in the stock room a lot ay the time. The only doonside wis the customers. Whit goat me was how stupit they were. They'd get you goin through aw your boaxes ay electric blankets tae see if you'd goat a green wan. Ah mean, it's no as if you're gonnae hing it on the waw. But if you telt them that they'd get dead minty, like, like they were fuckin royalty and no white trash fae Livvy at aw. And then they'd keep comin in wi' stuff that wis broken, like ah wis fuckin meant tae fix it. There was this wan posh wumman's came in wi' a radio, and ah wis dead guid wi' her, ah pit in new batteries an' everythin, but it still didnae work and ah even took the back aff it, and we looked at it for a while, and she's got pure impatient and she says to me, 'Do you not know what's wrong with it?', and ah says, 'Aye, ah dae, it's fucked, wifie.' Obviously, ah wis bein ironical, but she

84

kindae went raj and the manager fancied me and he was dead jealous that ah wis pumpin the van driver so ah got the boot and that wis the end ay ma brilliant career."

"Bastards."

"Here, you could easy get a proper job, though. You've been tae university."

"Aye, mehbe. Eh dinneh ken whit eh'd deh, though."

"You could always dae geography."

"Aye, but what does that mehn?"

"Well, you could draw maps, or you could be a geography teacher, or you could be a kind ay expert on the telly, like, people could come tae you and say, 'Whit's that?,' and you could say, 'It's a hill,' and they'd go, 'Thanks. There's a tenner.'"

"Yeah. But what would eh deh efter that?"

"Christ. D'ye want me to wipe yer erse for you? You'd go hame, hae your tea, watch the TV, tak the dug for a walk, pit yer bairns tae bed, and wash your motor and gie yer wife a seein-tae and hae a couple ay pints wi' yer mates at the weekend."

"That's just it. It's no enough. No once you've ridden a wehve."

As the Surfer did his best Byronic stare into the mid-distance, what he witnessed was the return of the Waltzer Monkey. This had not escaped the others' attention either. He pushed through and addressed the Surfer. "Ho, Norrin, you winchin ma herry, ya wee bawbag? Will ya ever fuckin get 'em in afore ah boot yer scrawny wee ginger erse fae here tae Rothesay."

Bob broached the $64,000 question. "Well?"

"Well whit? Suffice tae say, it's time for refuellin." He reached into his inside coat pocket and slipped the bag of sulphate into Bob's hand.

Dave was prepared to be impressed. "Come on, man, spit it oot. Did you get 'em or nae?"

The Monkey thrust his hand into another inside coat pocket and left it there. "Anybody care for a small wager?"

Bob couldn't take the tension. "Fuck's sake, Johnny!"

"Sha-fuckin-zam!" With a flourish he produced five tickets like he was slapping down a winning poker hand. He put an arm round the Mermaid. "You *shall* go to the ball, Cinders."

Bob McMillan was impressed. "Nivver doubted you for a moment, Monkey Man."

The Silver Surfer was impressed. "Teckle, Johnneh! How the fuck did you manage that?"

Dave Bruce was impressed. "How much wis it?"

"Fiver each, includin commission."

"Aye, OK, fair enough, I suppose. How *did* you manage it, by the way?"

"As luck would have it, the bouncer's cousin worked on the travellin shows wi' me. Bampot wiz oan the chair-o-planes. It's no whit you know, like they say."

Half an hour later and they were in. The Selecter weren't on yet, but the place was buzzing. They got down near the front as the band arrived on stage, and from the first beat the blue touchpaper was lit and the whole bastard box of fireworks went off. Just kept getting better and better. There were a few people up the back who weren't dancing, but not many, the place was fucking jumping. In the back of his mind, Bob knew the comedown would be hideous, but for now, thank Christ, the Monkey kept the chemical coming and he kept the drinks flowing.

The Selecter were smart and sharp, a totally two-tone experience. The lassie up front was too cool for school, looked sexy as fuck in a man's suit and hat, and the whole band were wired straight to the National Grid. When they finished the four lads and the Mermaid, howling like baboons, bounced about, arms round each other. Over the din, Dave Bruce could be heard. "Disnae get much better 'an 'is!"

But it did. As the next band came on, the *cognoscenti*, the fancy dress youth and a few old-school skinheids, went bonkers, and joined in as one of the six lads, all white boys this time, in a cheap suit and cheap shades, harangued them through a mic with more echo on it than a cheap horror movie.

And it all kicked off, like the crowd and the band were one daft sweaty thing. The Monkey grabbed Dave and yelled in his ear. "Worth a fiver, big man?"

Dave grinned and nodded, dancing like a bennied bear with a beefy dangerous-looking skinhead lassie next to him.

Halfway through the set Bob slipped the Silver Surfer a couple of quid. "Get 'em in, Norrin, eh?" As he queued at the bar the Surfer felt a mild unease, which, by the time he was leaning on the counter trying to get the staff's attention, had turned into an absolute imperative. Pushing his way back through the thirsty citizens behind him, he fought his way across the dancefloor, banged through the door of the gents and then into a stall, and dropping to his knees not a moment too soon, cowked his guts up into the shunky.

Fuck, that was close! What a relief! The noise of the gig seemed other-worldly as he pulled himself up on to the seatless porcelain. Christ, he just needed a couple of minutes here. Pishing with cold sweat, his teeth were grinding like bastards, his fucking heid was exploding. Deep breaths, calm the fuckin fuck doon. In his hurry, there had been no thought of locking the cubicle. The big lad who smashed the door open was sporting the full suit, pork pie hat and shades ensemble. Also two-tone shoes, the Surfer noted in the split second before he realised that the stranger's reason for being here, and the urgency of his visit, were identical to his. The large figure's arms reached forward and he supported himself on the wall behind the Surfer's head, looming over him. From the depths of his soul, animal noises built in volume, the prelude to a technicolour yawn of epic proportions. With inexorable drunken logic, the interloper anticipated his victim's likely irritation with the turn of events and took the precaution of punching his lights out.

Madness finished, and as the DJ played 'Skinhead Train' and the roadies started changing the gear around and things calmed down a bit, Bob McMillan had a question. "Far's Norrin?"

"Nae idea."

"Gave the sleekit fucker siller tae get 'e drinks in and he's disappeared wi't." He set off in pursuit with the righteous indignation of an Aberdonian who's been parted from his money. A tour round the dancefloor and bar revealed nothing. The gents was packed, but no sign of the wee ginger twally. Bob approached the shitehooses, and asked the question. "Norrin, ya in there?" There was no response. Some of the more helpful denizens of the cludgy riffed on the theme. "Norrin, ya in there?

Norrin, ya in there?! C'moan tae fuck, Norrin, there's folk gaggin' for a keech oot here!" Hopeless, and Bob was about to cross this line of enquiry off the list when he heard groans from the last stall. At the risk of embarrassment he gingerly tried the door, which swung open. What it revealed bore a passing resemblance to a pizza that's had a right good smack in the puss.

"For the love ay fuck, Norrin, fit the fuck's happened here?" The smell hit him and he gagged himself.

"Dinneh realleh ken... Jist sittin hehr... mindin meh ehn business... and then there was this... totalleh unprovoked... sorreh... Eh'll get the drinks in..." He attempted to rise, but slumped back down, abandoning the unequal struggle.

"I think there's a fair chance you winnae get served, mate. Gie's 'e cash." The two pound notes were still in the Surfer's hand, which he held out weakly. A small crowd of disgusted music lovers had now gathered behind Bob, torn between getting a good spot to see the Specials and the unstaged visceral human drama playing out before them. "Right, can you get up?"

"Eh think so... if you geh us a hand."

"Nae gonnae happen, Norrin. You'd understand if you were standin where I am."

"C'mon, man, eh dinneh... want... teh miss... the Specials."

"Once again, nae gonnae happen, you're a fuckin biohazard. Far you bidin these days?"

"Heh...market..."

"Be mair specific."

"84 Hehmarket… Terrace… second floor… on… the… left."

"Right, you're gonnae hiv tae hoof it hame. I'd gie you money for a taxi, but that's nae really an option either as the dice have rolled. We'll catch up wi' you there later, OK? You gonnae be alright?

"Dinneh ken… Jist let me… jist let me sit hehr… Eh've got a sehr fehce."

"That goes wi'oot sayin. Right, I'm gonnae get 'e drinks. See you up 'e road, eh?"

"Would you… close… the door?"

"Aye, sure. Lock it this time, eh. Think ay the children."

One of the spectators protested. "You cannae just leave him there like that!"

Bob answered on his way out. "He's a survivor." His return to the others with a tray of glasses coincided with the Specials' entrance and, as the band tore the place up, the only acknowledgement of the Surfer's existence as he staggered out of the building was an expression of distaste on fans' faces as they were briefly aware of the foul stench of the haggis and double sausage combo supper, pickled eggs and onions, and cherry trifles one of them had horsed a couple of hours earlier.

The Specials were something else. Hoofed the ball out the park. Like the other two bands they had the crowd in the palm of their hands, skanking like bastards, but there was a dark, confrontational, political vibe going on that took things to another level. The singer was a hoot, pale as a ghost, didn't crack a smile, didnae gie a fuck.

90

All too soon, it was over. As the DJ played old Trojan ska instrumentals, the place began to thin out a bit and Bob, Dave, The Mermaid and the Monkey retired, sweating, to the bar.

"Tell you fit, Johnny," said Dave, "I was wrang tae ivver doubt ye. A fiver well spent. In fact that may jist hiv been the best show ivver."

Contentious, and Bob questioned it. "Ziggy Stardust, Music Hall?"

"Aye, a classic, obviously, but nae 'e same, like. Maks a' the difference when you're up on your hind legs instead ay sittin in rows ay seats."

The Little Mermaid had just come to a realisation. "Where's the Surfer boy?"

"Somewhere between here and Haymarket, I hope."

"Eh? How come?"

"The exact chain of events is unclear, suffice to say I did find him. He wis covered in boak and somebody appeared tae hiv stoved his coupon in."

"Could he no jist have cleaned himsel up?"

"Na, it was in his hair an everythin."

"In his hair? How the fuck did he manage that?"

"Like I say, we're nae sure, but forensics are workin on it. I said we'd ging up tae his place and check on him."

The Monkey was unconvinced. "Will he have drink in?"

"Nae idea. Probably nae in sufficient quantities for this evenin's purposes."

"Haymarket, you say. Totally the wrang end ay toon."

"Fit you thinkin, Monkey Boy?"

"There's a wee bar doon in Leith. Normal licensin oors do not apply tae friends ay the management."

"Might you perhaps count yersel amang their number?"

"Definately worth a shottie. C'moan. Swallay and let's shoot the craw. The night is yet young."

On the way down Leith Walk, Dave Bruce was reminded briefly of a past life as they passed the Ford Escort. Present circumstances, however, were a more pressing concern. The amphetamine comedown was turning into a thing which would inevitably soon evolve into a horror show. "You got anither hit ay that whizz, Johnny?" he enquired, echoing the general unspoken sentiment.

The Mermaid concurred. "Aye, twa up, Johnny."

And Bob. "Mak 'at three, min."

"Naw, pure ripped it aw, troops." He looked around at the desperate gnashing faces. "However, as they used tae say in the B.B.s, 'Be Prepared'."

"Was that nae the Scouts?"

"They used tae tell us that in the Girl Guides 'n'aw."

"You were nivver in the Girl Guides, were you, Little Mermaid."

"Aye, how wid ah no be?"

"Nae reason. Jist disnae seem… Ken…"

"Goat ma joatters, right enough."

"Fit for?"

"Burnt doon the Guide hut."

"Right… onywey, you were sayin, Johnny?"

The Monkey reached into another inside pocket of his coat and came up with a bottle of pills. "The doctor is in! Ah'd say wan for a start, plenty mair where that came from if that's no enough."

"That is the coat that keeps on givin, man!"

By the time they wandered into the streets of the waterfront, deserted save for a couple of hooers on the corners, things had calmed down to the extent that Bob couldn't feel his feet. The Monkey did his ward rounds. "We aw feelin better?"

"Loose as a goose, amigo! Fit is 'at stuff?"

"Ah'm no exactly sure. Ma supplier said it worked oan hoarses, but. Now, it's roond here somewhere." Down a sidestreet, a dim light glowed from a shop with a Sweetheart Stout sign swinging. They approached quietly and listened at the window. Muffled voices indicated the presence of intelligent life. "Right, you boys zip it and hing oot in the shadows, you come wi' me, Kelly doll. Let me dae the talkin, aw you've got tae dae is look sexy." He unzipped her tracksuit top down to the navel.

"Whit you daein?"

"Trust me, have I ever let you down?" He knocked and waited. A ground floor window opened.

A flushed face with milk bottle specs topped off with a wispy comb-over emerged. "Ho, darlin, you're new, eh? Guid night?"

The Monkey took over. "No bad, Jim. She's done braw. Here, pal, got a couple ay chinas doon fae Aberdeen. That OK?"

"Lang as the tight bastards buy me a dram." The window closed, a couple of bolts clanked, and a rat-faced youth let them in.

At first glance, Bob remarked that what they appeared to have entered was a specialist area of Dante's Inferno. There could be no doubting the profession of the womenfolk, or that the menfolk largely performed a Svengali role in their commercial lives. While the others colonised a table Bob oozed over to the bar. Normally, he might have been a bit nervous in these unfamiliar surroundings, but the pony pill was doing its stuff and he felt at one with all creation, present company included. With what he assumed to be a winning grin, he included the sleazeball barman in the shout and, despite his lack of feet, delivered the drinks successfully.

The hours slid by in an agreeable haze. The Little Mermaid's annoyance at the casting decision which had been their ticket in was tempered by a blissed-out euphoria usually only experienced by a mare in labour. As a newcomer, she was the object of some interest from her supposed colleagues, but there was a large turnover of clientele as the phone behind the bar kept ringing and the ladies went out and about plying their ancient trade, and no unpleasantness.

A side-effect of the change in prescription was the return of Dave's appetite. Realising he hadn't eaten since that afternoon, he made up for lost time to the admiration of the assembled company and the barman by cleaning the place out of crisps and nuts. The Mermaid talked of crime and punishment, about her wee brother, currently languishing in Saughton after shooting Jehovah's Witnesses with an airgun and then lobbing a drain cover at them, and about her wee stretch in the Young Offenders following her flirtation with fire-raising. Bob, perhaps inspired by the veterinary medication, told the story of Rag Doll the racehorse, and its pivotal role in their all being there. The Waltzer Monkey was uncharacteristically silent.

"You OK there, Johnny?"

"Aye, I'll be fine. Took two ay them. Tell you whit, wouldnae pit money on masel' for the 3.30 at Kempton. Gie's a minute, alright."

The Mermaid wasn't prepared to comply. "C'moan, penny for your thoughts."

"50p."

"20p and that's ma final offer."

"Done."

"Can I pit it oan the slate?"

"Seeing as it's you."

"Well?"

"Ach, nothin really. Just stuff back hame. Borin work shite."

"You never telt me you'd a job."

"Aye, well, me and some pals've got a bit ay business goin, but."

"Whit sort ay business?"

"Buyin and sellin. Know what I mean. We've got an arrangement wi' this guy. I was at the school wi' his nephew. Mental, man. He's got this gaff, middle ay Govan, tenement flat, and he's done the place up like a palace, it's like Las Fuckin Vegas. The boy's done alright for himsel, right. Jist he's a bittie pissed aff wi' me."

"Is he like your godfather?"

"Eh?"

"Ken, like the fat boy in the film. Luca Brazzi sleeps wid da fishes, like."

"Aye, sort ay."

"That must be terrible."

"Whit?"

"Wakin up in bed wi' your hoarsie's heid. Ah wis greetin at that bit. It wisnae the hoarse that had dishonoured the boy's family. Did you dishonour your femmly, is that it?"

"No really."

"Ah dishonoured ma femmly. Aw the time. But they never did nothin like that tae me. We didnae even hae a hoarse. We hid an Airedale. Couldnae have cut its heid aff. Pure psycho, man. It would've hid your heid aff first. It got taken awaw intae care the ither day, cos it kept shitin itsel, aboot the same time as my brither, but it was ma wee pal. Ah think they've killed it, ah dinnae ken if they really take dugs intae care…"

Dave interrupted. "So how come the boy's pissed aff wi' you?"

"Aye, right, so he's gone oot tae take care ay a couple ay clients, and he's telt me and ma mates tae keep an eye on the place, so we're jist sittin aboot watchin his videos and gettin slowly aff wir coupons when the phone goes, and it's the big tip-aff, right. PC Plod is on his way as we speak. So, no time tae lose. We've got two big problems tae sort oot. Wan, the guy's got half a chemist's shop in the place, and I'm no talkin about the toothbrushes, and two, he's got a leopard, which you're no strictly meant tae have in Govan."

"A leopard? Yer arse!"

"Aye, went by the name ay John Greig. The leopard, that is."

The Mermaid was concerned. "Christ, did it no scratch his furniture tae fuck?"

"Aye, well, the guy used tae lob a load ay hash in its food tae keep it cool, which kind ay worked, but it pure improved its appetite n'aw. There wis claw marks on the fridge door, right enough, and when he took it oot at night it jist went mental for snacks. Went through a bin liner in ten seconds flat, take the fish supper from oot yer hauns as soon as look at ye, and ye cannae reason wi' a dope-crazed leopard. All came tae a heid when it ate the poodle doonstairs."

The Mermaid was fascinated. "Jesus, I would've jist legged it, me."

"The thought did cross wir minds, but we had a kindae moral responsibility tae sort things out for the boy."

"Fuck that!"

"Also, he would've found us and broken wir legs if we hadnae."

"Fair enough."

"So, there's a bit ay panic gaun on, but I kindae take charge, and I mind him tellin us he'd just bought a Jaguar."

The Mermaid was confused. "Christ, who is this guy, David fuckin Attenborough?"

"Naw, the car, like. OK. I find the keys in the lobby. Dancer! Meanwhile, I've got ma mates stuffin the gear intae boxes, cases, binbags, anythin, know whit I mean?"

"Fit aboot 'e leopard?"

"Right. Now, I get on OK wi' the leopard, but I've never tried tae get it tae go anywhere it didnae want tae go before. The other guys arenae even fuckin entertainin the idea ay dealin wi' this, so I get them tae take the stash doon intae the close and I wrap a couple ay valiums in a bit ay steak. No bother, straight doon the gregory like a dug eatin beetroot, spotty bastard thinks it's Christmas. It's got a chain thing round its neck, so I kindae gie it a wee pull, and, what d'ye know, it doesnae bite ma leg aff, it gets up and starts rubbin itsel against it. The steak's done the trick and John Greig thinks I'm made ay chocolate, like, he probably thinks I'm takin him oot tae mug punters for their chips or chase zebras or some shite, but, whatever's gaun on in his napper he's aw for it, know what I mean. I've got the mental munchies masel', so I grab some snacks for the road. Doonstairs, the car isnae so hard tae find, bein the only brand new XJS 4 litre coupé wi' a Union Jack an' Reid Haun ay Ulster paintjob on the street at that point. We load up the shite, like. There's a few weans hingin aboot, but naebody bats an eyelid, like they see punters wi' large African predators on a chain every day ay the week, which they probably do, as it goes. John Greig's no keen at first, but I lob some crisps intae the back seat, and the greedy cunt's in like a fuckin shot. We pile in. Wee snag. None ay us can really drive. Wance again, I take charge. I get the thing gaun. I pit my fit tae the floor and we're aff like like a greyhoond oot the traps and of course the stupid fuckin bizzies pick that very moment tae arrive in the opposite direction. Whammo fuckin bammo! Say whit you like about British engineerin but we've barely got a scratch, man. Meanwhile their front's pure stoved in, there's steam everywhere and the plod are pilin oot the motor. I pit ma fit doon again, and we're aff, and the polis are divin oot the way, and afore you can say 'Get tae fuck, Starsky, and your daft mate 'n'aw,' we're roond the corner and headin for the hills. Now, the guy's got a bit ay a lock up in Tradeston, and I've noticed there's some extra keys on the ring wi' the car keys, so I figure if there is a God and he cares aboot us we nash over there, stash the gear and the leopard, dump the motor somewhere and walk away withoot a stain on wir characters, end ay story. So we're aff across the Sooth Side as fast as our wee legs can carry us. The sun's shinin and God's a proddie. First problem. The leopard disnae like the guy sittin beside him. The punter's just no good wi cats, y'understaun. John Greig's probably jist bein playful, like, but I look in the mirror and I can see things are gettin slightly oot ay haun, the boy's already in a bit ay a mess. I also notice we've got company. Mair cops, coming up fast on wir tail. I remember the boy used tae sing 'The Sash' tae the leopard and it used tae seem tae kind ay like it, so I get us aw singin. Meanwhile the filth fire up the siren, so between that and 'The Sash' and the leopard roarin and my mate in the back screamin you cannae fuckin hear yersel think. We're hoorin up the Paisley Road West at this point and the Old Firm game's jist comin oot and the Bears have won and the punters are cheerin us as we go by and gettin in the way ay the cop car and the boy in the back's a pape and it's like his worst fuckin nightmare has become flesh. John Greig is up tae his knees in Fenian blood."

"Dae leopards have knees?"

99

"Couldnae swear tae it"

"I think they dae."

"I beg tae differ. Nae like us onywey."

"Mebbe we'll never know. OK. We've given the polis the body swerve for the moment and we find the place in Tradeston, and we've got the right keys an everythin. The two ay us get the goods in there. I grab the leopard. I sling some Peperamis intae the back ay the lock-up and he's in there like fuckin slippy lightnin. Jist then we hear the sirens doon the road. We've got a problem here. The lane the lock-up's in's a deid end. No way out. We pull what's left ay the left-fitter oot the back. We jink up a close but it's only a matter ay time before they find us. The constabulary arrive. I take a quick butcher's round the corner. Three Pandas. It's no lookin good. They hover aboot the Jag for a while, glaikit-like, then they see the open lock-up and bugger me if aw six ay the cunts dinnae stroll straight in. Too good tae miss. I've shut the door and got the padlock back on afore the fuckers can say 'Foxtrot Alpha tae Control'. We'd have loved tae stay longer. We did hear wan ay them say, 'Watch oot, there's a big fuckin dug in here,' and John Greig havin a bit ay a growl, but when you gottae go, you gottae go. So, up tae the road, hop in a taxi, drop the Tim aff at the hospital, and on tae the Masonic Arms for tea and scones."

"So fit's happened tae 'e boy wi' 'e leopard?"

"Last I heard he's free as a bird. The polis didnae have a search warrant for the lock-up, so he's aff on a technicality, but the leopard's banged up on GBH in Calderpark Zoo at Her Majesty's Pleasure. Guy's got all sorts ay plans tae spring it, though, and I wouldnae pit it past him."

Bob looked at his watch. "Christ, it's nearly four o'clock. We should get wirsels up 'e road and check on 'e Silver Surfer, man. He was in some fuckin state, like."

The Monkey lacked enthusiasm. "Fucked if I'm hoofin it aw the way up tae Haymarket. Dinnae even ken if I can get oot this seat."

"We'll get a taxi. It's on Rag Doll."

Johnny managed to persuade their unprepossessing host to sell them a cairry-oot, and they hopped in a cab at the foot of the Walk. The door of the Surfer's flat was opened by a posh-sounding, camp-looking Chinaman. "Good evening, the master has been expecting you," he intoned, and held the door open for them.

In a surprisingly tastefully-appointed old-fashioned living room there was Norrin, bruised but undefeated, sitting at a huge mahogany table by the window with two lassies, in a tartan dressing gown drinking cocoa like nothing had occurred. "Hi, eh was wonderin what had happened teh you. This is Shona and Carol and that's Richard. We're plehin Dungeons and Dragons. Eh'd invite you teh join in, but it would be a bitteh complicated at this stehge. Only one hoose rule. Coasters if you're using the big tehble. The landlord's no happy wi 'us even hehin it, but he'd heh teh dismantle it teh get it oot the door."

"You've cheered up since I last seen you."

"Aye, gutted eh missed the Specials, though." And the Surfer cheered everybody up by relating the strange tale of the queasy yet psycho kid-on rude boy who had brought his evening to such an unexpected conclusion. "Tell you what, though, dinneh ken how eh'm gonneh get teh sleep toneht. Still hummin' like a power stehtion, man."

The others looked knowingly at each other and the Waltzer Monkey produced a pill. "Road-tested and approved."

"What is it?"

"Better than cocoa. Now, drinkies, boys and girls?"

"Be rude not to."

The Monkey handed out tins of beer and passed round a half bottle of Bell's. The flatmates thought better of trying to catch up and headed off to their beds. Shona pointed sternly at the Surfer as she exited. "I'm holding you responsible," was her parting shot.

Norrin poured some whisky into his hot chocolate and took a slug to wash down the donkey dope. "Sounds, pop pickers?"

"Aye, dinnae pit ony shite on."

Norrin did no such thing. The choice was Curtis Mayfield, *Superfly*. The smooth soul-jazz and the zebra zonkers were a perfect combination and the crack was laid back and witty and *a propos* of nothing at all until Dave broke the spell. "Tell you fit, I'm nae gonnae lie tae you, I'm fuckin Hank."

The Mermaid was incredulous. "You've jist eaten every crisp and peanut in a hale bar, ya big gannet!"

"Gottae keep my strength up, darlin." He looked hopefully at the Surfer.

"Eh've jist got Jehcobs' Crehm Crackers and lehm marmalehd, but there's a behkery back doon at the cross thehr." He looked at his watch. "If you go in about the back door, theh'll heh stuff behked beh now."

"You're kiddin me. I love this place!" And singing the bit from 'New York, New York' about waking up in a city that never sleeps, he was out the door.

The Surfer noticed that the Little Mermaid was yawning and turned to Johnny. "Where you behdin the neht, beh the weh?"

"We hadnae made any plans, but…"

Norrin strained his numbed brain to hatch a scheme whereby the Monkey ended up elsewhere and the Mermaid ended up with him, but all that was forthcoming after an embarrassing silence was, "Yiz can crash on the couch if you want, eh suppose."

Dave Bruce returned with greasy paper bags and the Surfer spread newspaper on the table. The others' appetite was beginning to return and their interest was piqued. "Whit you got, big man?"

"Fit hiv I nae got!" Pies, sausage rolls, bridies, cream horns, iced fingers and a jam sponge spilled forth, and Dave stuck in with gusto. "'Is is fuckin braw," he announced through a mouthful of macaroni pie, "Fresh oot the oven. Help yersels."

"I'd advise you nae tae hing aboot," Bob suggested. "He'll hae the lot." The others scavenged around the edges of the large youth's feeding frenzy like small birds round a savannah predator.

When it was all over, Dave Bruce collapsed back in his seat. "I dinnae ken aboot ony good ideas you've hid in the past, Norrin, but that's gottae be een ay your best. So fit's a'body daein' 'e morn?"

The Monkey was already all over it. "We shouldnae plan too far ahead at this stage. We're gonnae meet in Stewart's at 1.30 and take it fae there. That's assumin you grippy sheep fanciers are gaun somewhere else in the interim?"

"Ay, Christ, we've paid for 'e hotel room, Brucie, we should heid back and get wir money's worth."

And so it came to pass that Bob and Dave made their way beneath the castle along an eerily deserted Princes Street as the stars faded and Saturday dawn began to break clear and crisp. The Little Mermaid had already passed out in her chair and the Surfer took his leave. His bedroom was next to the sitting room and as he lay in his scratcher, contemplating whether his cheekbone was broken and horny as a stoat, he heard the Monkey's voice and the Mermaid's sleepy response, then *sotto voce* conversation and laughter, followed in remarkably short order by the unmistakeable sounds of sexual congress.

In the lobby of the North British Hotel, Dave Bruce sniffed the air. "Fuck me, if I'm nae very much mistaken they've started servin breakfast."

"Are you serious?"

"Have you ivver kent me nae tae be in matters ay this kind? Come awa', min, it's included."

"Since you pit it like 'at..."

# 19

Stewart's Bar lay far enough from both Easter Road and Tynecastle that you didn't get a significant fitba clientele, but it was busy nonetheless. Bob was delighted to see the old juggling barman was still earning an honest buck and on sparkling form. "Two pints ay Mick Jagger it is, boys," and a glass spun over the top of his head from behind his back. He caught it, right way up, just before it smashed on the counter, as the second glass popped up above the bar from between his legs and was snatched out of the air and smacked down beside its mate.

About a quarter to two, the Monkey, the Mermaid and the Surfer, his bruise now resplendent in all the colours of the rainbow, straggled in.

Bob viewed the dishevelled arrivals with a grin. "Fit like, 'en, citizens?"

"Me and the Mermaid are brand new. Somebody's pished on Norrin's fireworks, but."

"There's fuck all wrang wi' me!" Though, in all fairness, he had a right face on him.

The Monkey wouldn't let it lie. "Fuck's sake, man, there's nae point mopin about it."

"Eh'm no mopin, reht. 'Mope, mope, mope,' that's somebody that's mopin. About what, anyweh."

"I dinnae ken. Suit yersel."

Over a couple of pints they discussed tactics. Having largely failed the day before, the Mermaid had her heart set on shopping. The Aberdonians weren't keen and the Surfer was still in the huff, but the Monkey argued that, if they were in this for the duration, a wee break from the sauce would be vital. And so they found themselves in the Grassmarket with the Little Mermaid's face in the window of a second-hand clothes joint. "This is quality. Ah'm gaun in."

Bob's eyes were drawn to an establishment across the way bearing the name O. McGreevy, Turf Accountant. "Tell you fit, Little Mermaid. While you're in there, the lads might pye a wee visit tae Mr. Mac over 'e road? Fit div you think the O stands for?"

"Otto."

"I hope you're right."

The 3.30 at Aintree was the next one up, eleven runners in a steeplechase. Following his recent good fortune, Robert McMillan's advice was sought. He tried to steer them in the right direction, but the Surfer was having none of it, opting for Tangerine Dream, which, as far as Bob could see, had nothing to recommend it to the discerning punter, either in terms of odds or form. And yet cantered home while Dave's fell on its arse, the Monkey's lost interest and Bob's jockey hit the ejector seat button at the second fence. The losers opted to join the Mermaid, but Norrin, though a bit cheerier, not to say smug since his win, preferred his own and Otto's company for the moment.

In the vintage shop, the Mermaid had got her feet under the table. The geezer who ran the place was having a cup of tea with her as a couple of American lassies tried stuff on. One of them came out in a cocktail dress and checked herself in the mirror. "Whaddya think, honey?"

"Colour suits ye, but a bittie tidy roon' yer airse," was the Mermaid's candid assessment through a mouthful of Penguin.

"Excuse me?"

Her pal replied from the changing room. "I guess she's saying your butt's too big, Candy."

"Naw, it's no yer bahoochie as such, it's jist cut for a racin snake, like."

"That's genuine Chanel," the proprietor protested.

The Mermaid was unimpressed. "Well, she was haein an aff-day. You could aye get it altered, but I wouldnae pay full whack for it. Gie her a discount, Fred."

"Another discount!" He sighed. "I tell you what, lads, I'm robbing myself here."

The second lass came out from behind a curtain wearing a tartan miniskirt and gave it a twirl. She looked over at the Mermaid who grinned and gave her a big thumbs-up. "And this is the genuine Goldberg plaid, right?" she asked the shopkeeper.

"Absolutely. Hunting Goldberg, to be precise. One of the more *recherché* patterns. Not something you'd find in the tourist shops."

"I'll take it."

This went on and on, and then, as it seemed to the lads, on a bit more. As the girls finally got changed and Fred packed up their purchases and totted up the bill, Dave took a white-banded fedora down off a shelf and tried it on, to the amusement of the Monkey. "You look like Al Capone, big man!"

"DON'T CALL ME SCARFACE! Fit d'ye think?"

"Suits you." The Little Mermaid nodded her approval. "You should definately buy it."

"How much?"

"Normally a tenner, but since you're a friend of Kelly's, we'll call it eight."

"Gie you a fiver for it."

"That's a collector's piece, son: 1930s. Couldnae go lower than seven fifty."

"Six pound, Fred, and that's the absolute limit of my hat budget today…"

"I'm a fool to myself. Go on, then."

Dave looked over at Bob. "I'll pye ye back."

With a deep sigh, Bob parted with the readies as the Yank girls returned to the shop floor. Fred hoyed several big bags up on the counter. "Now, ladies, that comes to a total of £250."

"American Express?"

"That'll do nicely."

They filled out travellers' cheques and bade their adieus. When they'd disappeared from in front of the window, Second-Hand Fred danced out from behind the counter and swept the Mermaid up in an old-fashioned waltz. "If I ever need an assistant, Kelly darling, I will look no further. That noise you just heard, gentlemen, was the happy sound of money and old rope changing hands. I hope you were paying attention. You see anything you fancy, doll?"

The Mermaid had only had her eye on one thing since she walked in the shop, a slim-cut black silk Chinese jacket embroidered with a red dragon. It had seen better days, but she was blind to any deficiencies. She pointed. "How much?"

"See if it fits you first."

The answer was, 'Like a glove.' When she came out of the changing room the World of Suzie Wong vibe caused a marked testosterone spike. The fact that it was a wee bit scruffy just made it sexier. The Mermaid looked at herself in the mirror and burst into bitter sobs.

"What's up?"

"It's… too… bonny… who am ah kiddin?… It's no for me… Ah'm jist a new toon mink… Ah dinnae even hae ony money… I should never have come in here…"

Fred and the Monkey exchanged glances. The second-hand man flipped the full-strength professional switch as he stepped forward, placed his hands on the Mermaid's upper arms and stood her up straight. "Right, first thing, you're too bonny for the jaicket, no the other way round. I've had this shop for thirty year, and I shouldn't tell you this, but it's never the claes, it's who's wearing them." And then performed a handbrake turn into the amateur. "You've made me about two hunner quid this afternoon, it's a present."

As the tears flowed and the Mermaid hugged the vintage clothes man and the lads didn't know where to look, in came the Surfer, his mood transformed.

"Otto get his money back, then?" the Monkey asked.

Norrin shook his head. "Quite the reverse. Otto McGreevy 0-Silver Surfer 3."

"Ya jammy bastard!"

"Aye, but here's the best bit. It's an omen."

"Fit?"

"First winner-Tangerine Dream."

"Aye."

"Second winner-Terror's Destiny. Third winner-Arabesque"

"Na, you've lost me."

"D'ye no seh? Who's at Pittodreh the deh?"

"Dundee United. We've already discussed this at some length, and established that youse bastards are gonnae get a right cuffin aff the Mighty Dons." Dave looked at his watch. "On that subject, we need tae find a boozer wi' a TV almost immediately." They took their leave of Fred and crossed the Grassmarket to The Last Drop. As they got the order in, the English Second Division was just coming through. Bob and Dave felt the trepidation that any fan feels, but Fergie's Aberdeen feared no-one that season. To be fair, the Arabs were a handy team as well, but at Pittodrie? Surely not. The refreshments were handed round, and the suspense ramped up as the fates of Tranmere Rovers, Port Vale and other obscure yet magical names were invoked.

The screen flipped and they saw it before it was announced.

Aberdeen 0-Dundee United 3. The Surfer went raj. "Get it up yiz, ya sheepshaggin' hooers! I telt ye it was an omen!"

The Monkey was also elated as the results rolled: 'Kilmarnock 2-Celtic 0; Rangers 2-Partick Thistle 1'. "Immaterial, as you see, Norrin. The Teddy Bears are back, man." The only consolation the Aberdonians could derive, as the prospect of another false dawn opened up before them, was that they'd come to Edinburgh instead of going down the Merkland Road. "Face it, boys, there's only wan real fitba city in Scotland. It's no like either ay youse bastards are ever gonnae win European trophies. It's no like Bayern Munich and Real Madrid and Barcelona and that are quakin in their boots aboot whit happens at Pittodrie or Tannadice."

This arrogance forged a sudden and unexpected solidarity among the East Coasters. The Surfer, flushed with the afternoon's wins, spoke. "Fehfer, then, Johnneh."

"Eh?"

"Fehfer says ehther Dundeh United or Ehberdeen win a European cup in the next ten years and the Hun dinneh."

"Yer arse!"

"No, deadleh sehrehous. Yeh fehrt, Monkeh Man?"

"Aye, that'll be right! Bring it on, Norrin. Just feel like I'm robbin you." The Surfer spat on his hand and slapped it down on Johnny Barr's. "You boys fancy a bit ay this action as well?" An innate financial prudence, coupled with the dire news from the shadow of the gasometer, led them to pick discretion over valour. "How about you, Kelly doll?"

"Ah dinnae like fitba. Went tae see the Shire wance. Load ay

111

shite. Only thing ah'd bet on is they're never gonnae win sweet fuck all."

The Monkey had already moved on. "We up for a fly yin in the Tabs?" He was proposing a short stroll up the shadowy Cowgate to the Nips of Brandy, often referred to as the Tabs of Acid owing to its secondary function, and there they found themselves, in a bar where day and night lost their meanings. While the others shot the breeze round a table, Johnny Barr absented himself for a conversation with Scouse Charlie, a sallow, pudgy man, of indeterminate age with no neck and long curly hair like a shite version of Captain Hook, who nobody could recall seeing in daylight. The others watched proceedings discreetly but with interest. Charlie was a person you were acquainted with, largely through his habit of turning up uninvited late at night wherever there was a light on and not leaving, but you wouldn't go out of your way to seek his company. Many people knew him simply as 'The Moth', others as 'The Man They Couldn't Hang'. An unknown third party joined them. It was unlikely that Johnny Barr was hanging out with them just for the crack. After a while the Moth excused himself to the lavvy. A couple of minutes later the Monkey did likewise, followed by the stranger. He re-emerged shortly afterwards, picked up his pint and drained it. "C'moan, drink up and let's leg it afore he comes oot and bores the livin airse aff us."

Night had fallen. On the way up the hill past yet another Bobby, the Mermaid was intrigued. "Where we gaun noo?"

"Aye, Da, where you takin us?"

"The Meadows. Picnic."

"Whit's the Meadows?

"A picnic? It's cauler than a witch's airse and we hinnae got ane ay thae baskets. You got ootside caterers comin in?"

"It's no the kind ay picnic where you need scran. Jist 360-degree views."

"Fit you on aboot?"

"I think you'll be pleasantly surprised." As, indeed, Scouse Charlie had been with one of the be-cool-mule pills. So pleasantly surprised, it turned out, he'd bought the whole bottle, leaving the Monkey with a tidy profit in cash, plus a few little extras. They sat down under a full moon bang in the middle of the open country between George Square and the headlights sweeping along Melville Drive, and, as indistinct figures made their way along the paths in the mid-distance, he half-unwrapped a thin foil package, took a long, hard sniff, and passed it round.

"Mmmm... nice. What have we here, garcon?"

"La crème de la crème, monsieur. Thai stick. I guarantee you winnae get anythin better than this in the whole ay Scotland right now." The Monkey skinned up and they sat shivering on and smoking the grass, in a watchful silence broken by the Surfer giggling quietly at first, then convulsing on the ground.

"Oh Chrehst, help. Somebodeh help me. Somebodeh plehse help me!"

"Fasiboy?"

"Is he gonnae be alright, do we think?"

The crack-up was infectious and came in waves. Just when it seemed to be subsiding somebody else would go.

Eventually Dave got words out. "Jesus H. Christ, what is this shit?"

"I telt you, it's a Thai stick," the Monkey explained as he rolled another one.

"How can any of us know in essence why anything is whatever shit it is, though, really?" mused Bob.

"Well, like, I suppose cos it's a stick and it comes fae Thailand." They digested this information for a moment, before the Surfer lost it again.

"Fit's up wi' you now?"

"Cos he said 'It's a stick and…'" It was no good. He rolled on the cold grass.

The Mermaid looked around her with trepidation. "It's pure spooky oot here. Do you think there's werewolves?"

Bob sought to reassure her. "Dinnae imagine so."

"How do you know I'm no a werewolf?"

"Cos you're a monkey. Ye dinnae get Scottish werewolves. Although, c'm'ere, there was a movie, couple ay years back, *Legend of the Werewolf*, if I'm nae mistaken. Boy that played the werewolf wis fae Aiberdeen.

The Mermaid both confirmed and doubted Bob's assertion. "Ah seen that. He was never fae Aberdeen. I dinnae even think he was Scottish."

"Na, he is. I read it in the Evenin Express."

114

"Must be true, then."

"Total fuckin ride, though, the boy!"

"Little Mermaid, I'm shocked."

"Hey, you could have entered that as a plea in mitigation fan you wis done for pishin against yon lamp-post, Bobby."

"Eh?"

"Sorry, your honour, time ay the month, ken."

"Lon Chaney Junior! He wis a werewolf n'aw."

"Fit aboot Lon Chaney Senior?"

"Na, dinnae think it's hereditary, lycanthropy. I think you jist need tae get bitten by a werewolf, but it's got tae stop short ay actually eatin you. Obviously. Or…"

A silence fell, broken only by the Surfer's muffled gibbering, as the second jeggie did the rounds.

Something had been bothering the Waltzer Monkey. "Lon, though, but? Whit's it short for?"

"I dinnae ken. Lonsdale?"

"Lonsdale?"

"Aye. Why nae?"

"I wish I wis cried Lonsdale."

"It could be arranged."

"Whit aboot you?"

"Raoul. Dave?

"Monty. Mermaid?"

"Mercedes."

"Like the car?"

"Aye, but it's the other way roon. He called the motor efter his wife or daughter or somebody."

"Fa?"

"Mr. Benz."

"Your heid is full ay unexpected shite, Mermaid."

"Ma da wis a mechanic… before. I ken aw aboot cars."

"Fit dis he dae noo?"

"He's in the hoaspital."

The Surfer surfaced. "Lonneh Donegan!"

"Oh, look out. He's back. What you on aboot noo?" the Monkey enquired.

"Another Lonsdehl. Eh was thinking, you dinneh get many people ca'd Lonsdehl, apart feh the Chehnehs, lehk?"

"Who the scary fuck's Lonnie Donegan?"

"You're kidding meh, Johnny. The king eh skiffle, man!"

"Where's Skiffle?"

"No whehr. What. The precursor of rock and roll. Without Lonneh Donegan, there is no Elvis Presleh."

Dave bridled. "'At's a very contentious statement. Some might even say a load ay bollocks."

"Eh stand by it."

"Outline your argument."

"Well, when Elvis was weh, lehk, him and Jerreh Leh Lewis and their mehts used teh sehcretly listen teh the black rehdio stehtions and snehk inteh the black music clubs, and it's thehr theh first heard and saw Lonneh Donegan and his washboard."

"This would have been where?"

"Memphis, Tennesseh."

"Uh-huh. So your position is that Lonnie Donegan is American?"

"Certainleh."

"And black?"

"As your fuckin hat."

"Aye, that'll be right! Are you for real, min? Fit a bunch ay utter shite! I can only say that your knowledge of the history of popular music is woefully sketchy and that I shall mak it a mission to demonstrate to you before I die that Lonnie Donegan was, in fact, a white British entertainer of the 1950s, veering towards vaudeville rather than rhythm and blues, who, while I grant you, was something ay a seminal influence on the early Beatles, or Quarrymen, probably did not touch Elvis's life even fleetingly." Dave stubbed the roach out violently.

Silence reigned once more, broken by the Mermaid. "Calm the fuck doon, Dave, eh."

Bob was familiar with the symptoms. "He gets like this when he's hungry. Tell you fit. Curry. Murder. Masel'. Totally fuckin could."

A wave of stoned unanimity engulfed them, as they upped the stakes.

"Aye, wi' poppadums!"

"Parathas!"

"Tarka dal!"

"Peshwari naan!"

"Na, keema naan, maan!"

"Baith!"

"Onion bhajis!"

"Mango chutney!"

"Chicken pakora!"

"Gottae be prawn puri!"

"Lashins ay lager!"

"All ay the above," enthused Dave. "Jist point me in the right direction."

"Starry?" suggested the Monkey.

"Nah. Khushi's. It's jist up 'e road."

"Setterday night? Might hae tae wait for a table at Khushi's."

"Himalehan?"

"Bittie pricey. C'moan, Starry's quality and cheap. Fifteen minutes and we're there if we hoarse it."

Bit of an underestimate, as it turned out. At the northwest end of the Meadows they found themselves on Lonsdale Terrace which necessitated a pause for wild speculation as to which Lonsdale it commemorated and the role of kismet in the weekend as a whole. Eventually Dave convinced them that the significance was that they were destined to follow this star to the Star of Bengal and they should get the finger out. The Surfer was coaxed down from a tree he'd decided to climb and the ever more urgent moonlit march continued.

In the restaurant they ordered with the abandon that the Thai stick demanded. Conversation by this stage was limited to fevered conjecture as to when the nosebag would show up and exactly how delicious it was going to be. The staff had, naturally, seen misjudged gluttony on this level many times before, but their devotion to profit was such that they weren't about to discourage it. They hadn't, of course, reckoned with Dave Bruce. As the drinks and dishes started arriving, a hush fell over the table broken only by sporadic expressions of pure stoner joy.

As the others reached capacity one by one and the big man

hoovered up, a team of lassies made their entrance, dressed to slaughter, and sat down near the door. Bob, facing them, had a flash of recognition. "Here, Monkey Man, dinnae look now, but 'at's Jane Cranston jist come in." Jane had studied law with Morag, been an object of lust for pretty much the entire male university population, and had a brief, ill-fated and explosive liaison with Johnny Barr.

In the Waltzer Monkey's shoes, Bob would have been a nervous wreck right about now, but, whether it was the grass or that old innate Glesca gallus thing, the Monkey's insouciance was admirable. "Book us a banana split, eh," and he was up, across the shop, helping himself to a chair and, by all appearances, charming the pants off the entire table within minutes.

Dave checked himself in a McEwan's mirror, adjusted the hat, and rose. "Peach melba for me, and a coffee," and he joined the other table and introductions were made and thumbnail autobiographies and patter exchanged. Bob contemplated joining in too, but didn't feel he could get away with abandoning the Mermaid and the Surfer and contented himself with an embarrassing wave across the room. She looked daggers over her shoulder, draped an arm round Norrin's neck and rested her head on his shoulder while his features conveyed delight and panic in equal measure and Bob got the dessert order in.

Puddings, coffees and After Eights showed up, the other two made their excuses and clocked back in, inordinately pleased with a job well done. "Gottae tell you, 'is loon is some fuckin operator," Dave enthused. "The rest ay the evenin appears tae be sorted oot, wid you nae say, Johnny?"

"Aye, lookin promisin, troops. Jane and her mates are awaw up tae Clouds later on, said we'd see them there…"

"… It's no Clouds eneh mehr," the Surfer corrected. "It's

Coasters, and it's a roller disco now. Eh'll be fehn, like, cos eh'm a surfer and eh've got natural balance, but…"

"Ay, fitivver, Norrin," Dave butted in, smiling across at the girls' table, "'e footwear's nae 'e primary consideration here. Yon quines look good enough tae eat."

Bob could not but agree. "Each one lovelier than the last, right enough. Although I cannae believe you're still hungry, Brucie."

"… And there's a perty. Doon the Canongate somewhere. Got the address. Meantime, since we're headed that way in any case, Bennet's?" The Monkey's suggestion was rubber-stamped, the bill was paid, and they made their way out.

"See you up the *strasse*, girls," was Johnny's parting shot.

"Gas meetin you, ladies. See you on 'e dancefloor," was Dave's.

Bob gave another lame wave as he exited. Jane smiled. "Hi, Bobby." But he was halfway out the door and engaging in conversation would have involved pushing back through the Surfer and the Mermaid and he was bereft of snappy one-liners. He opened his mouth like a fish. The table of girls giggled.

The Surfer attempted a stoned sexy smile but ended up looking like a serial killer. The Mermaid cut the other lassies dead, and they were off, following the smell of the brewery towards Tollcross, arguing about shortcuts and getting lost. At long last in Bennet's Bar, Dave tapped another fiver off Bob and got the order in. The barmaid smiled as she trayed the drinks up. "I like your hat."

"Thanks, jist got it today." Dave jauntified the angle in the mirror behind the bar and reflected that not only was she pretty, but the whole gaff was pretty splendid. And very well-stocked.

"Christ, how many whiskies you got there?"

"About three hunner."

"You tried 'em a'?"

"Dinnae even like it. I'm workin in the wrong place, eh."

"What *do* you like?"

"Hirondelle."

"Can I get you one?"

"Aye, go on then."

"Listen, we're goin dancin across the road later. You fancy comin?"

She held up her left hand. "Spoken for, Al Capone. Gottae get back tae ma bairn."

Dave smiled ruefully as she gave him his change. "Too much, too young!" A table had come free as they entered, and he dished the drinks out. "It's like nip nirvana in here. You seen the selection?"

"Famous for it."

The Surfer rose and returned with five large ones and a wee jug of water. "There weh go. It's on Otto and the cuddehs. Eh just got a mixture. You can treh and guess what theh are or you can just neck them."

"Good man, Norrin. Slainte!"

"Slainte, pals! Teh Jim McLehn!"

"Tae Jim McLean and his skelpit-airse puss!"

The Mermaid took a tentative sip. "Ah dinnae usually like whisky, but that's quite fine."

"These are all the real MacKeh, man." As the others savoured the internal glow, the Surfer swallowed in double quick time and returned from the bar with another one.

"Thirsty, Norrin?"

"Aye, this is demij, boys and girls. Eh'm gonneh go on a wee tour eh Scotland." And so he did. By express train. With added excursions to Newcastle upon Tyne. Come chucking-out time he was about a seven, ten being comatose and nine unable to form human words.

As they weaved their way between the Tollcross traffic and Coasters roller disco swam into focus, the Mermaid was concerned. "Whit's he gonnae be like on roller skates?" She needn't have worried. The *dénouement*, when it came, was swift, unforeseen, and decisive.

As they progressed up the queue, they could feel the doormen's eyes on them. When they reached the marquee, the Waltzer Monkey fronted up the operation. "Aye lads, how's it gaun?"

The bouncer was a brick shitehoose. "Nae trainers, boys. Sorry."

Bob saw a flaw in the logic. "Now, I'm nae bein smert here, but am I nae right in thinkin we're gonnae be wearing roller skates, so…"

"Nae trainers."

Impasse. Broken by the Surfer pushing his way to the front and slurring thus, "It's all very well for youse teh be hehr chucking folk oot, ya fat fanneh, while your wehf's at hehm sucking a darkeh's cock." The one was a neat uppercut which loosened his teeth, the two a powerhouse jab to the solar plexus. Dave Bruce swung a blocked right hook and got one in return that laid him out on the pavement, the doorman's signet ring opening up a cut above his eye for good measure, as the second bouncer arrived full tilt and hoofed him in the bollocks. The Surfer retreated, doubled-up, grabbed hold of the boy behind them in the queue for balance and lost the entire evening meal and a selection of cracking whiskies over his trousers. Understandably miffed at the surprise conclusion to his night out, the victim grabbed him by the hairstyle and booted a used-madras-stained brogue loafer repeatedly into his face. The Mermaid was at the stranger like a cat, claws out, drawing four neat lines of blood down his cheek. His girlfriend took a wild swing with her handbag, missed, slid on the vomit and landed on her arse in the middle of it. As a crowd gathered the blue flashing lights of a passing squad car lit up the scene, Bob grabbed Norrin, the Monkey peeled Dave off the footpath and retrieved the fedora, the Mermaid kicked Handbag Girl in the tits and they legged it down on to Lothian Road and kept pegging it raggedly into the backstreets of Fountainbridge until they finally collapsed wheezing in a dark wee alley.

The Monkey's voice broke through the panting. "Cannae believe you fuckin said that, Norrin, ya raj wee bawbag!"

"Jesus, did you check the quine skitin and landin clean on her jax in the cowk!" added Bob. "By the way, remind me nae tae pick a scrap wi' you, Little Mermaid. You fight dirty."

Kelly Reid had switched from Catwoman to Vatican Sculpture. She cradled the stricken Surfer in her arms. "No haein' too much luck this weekend, eh?"

He put a brave face on it. "Swings… and roondaboots, lehk… 3–0 at Pittodreh, man…" A weak smile revealed a couple of missing choppers.

Bob turned to his bloodstained buddy. "Fit like, Davie man?"

"Been better, Bobby. Aye got 'e hat, 'at's 'e main thing. Fit noo?"

The Monkey assessed the situation. "We're jist up the road fae Norrin's place, eh? Ah suggest we get the wee man back and regroup there."

At 84 Haymarket Terrace the Surfer's flatmates were out, they had the place to themselves. In five minutes he progressed through stages eight and nine and lay slumped catatonic in an armchair. A bit of detective work revealed a shrine to the dodgy apricot Arabs featuring a surfboard sketchily sprayed silver and they laid him out like a corpse and slung the quilt over him. A wake seemed appropriate and further sleuthing discovered the remains of the previous night's cairry-oot.

Dave surveyed the album collection. "He may ken fuck all aboot Lonnie Donegan, and maybe this is a' his mates' records, but I'm willin to gie him the benefit ay the doot and say there's some quality here."

"Dinnae pit ony shite on."

He put on *Raw Power* loud, and spirits lifted. The recent adrenalin rush was making the beer and whisky go down well. The Mermaid got up.

"Where you gaun?"

"Ah wis gaun tae the lavvy. But first I must dance for you." She jumped on the table as the Stooges kicked into 'Your Pretty Face is Going to Hell'. To add to the list of 'Things You Never Fully Realised About the Little Mermaid' was quite how good a mover she was. At first the lads contented themselves with hooting and hollering, then Bob McMillan joined her on the table. Followed by the Waltzer Monkey. Followed by Dave Bruce.

It was a solid old piece of furniture, but at that point a sped-up montage of chairs, jigsaws, heart-to-heart conversations, glassware, dinner parties, newspapers, board games, breakfasts, bottles, cutlery, crockery, cruet sets, late-night drinks, laughter, lunches, ten thousand teas and coffees, tears, tantrums, tablecloths and napkins through the ages, a fruitbowl and a few febrile fucks flashed before its eyes before the timbers creaked, cracked, split, and splintered, leaving the *corps de ballet* in a heap on the carpet.

Dave took out the turntable on his way down and the needle rasped across the vinyl. The crackly silence was deafening "Fuck. That's like antique, eh."

"Fuck is right. D'ye think we can fix it?" The others looked at Bob with incredulity.

The Mermaid shook her head. "No if you were the best jiner in the world, which ah'm guessin yer no, cos you jist asked that question."

The Monkey clutched at straws. "Mebbe we could just like make it look like it's no fucked, but, know what I mean."

Dave gestured at the crippled Victoriana. "Be ma guest, Johnny. We need tae wake Norrin up and tell him."

"Aye, or we could just leg it. I dinnae think the Surfer's in a

126

good place tae deal wi' this right now. Here's the Jackanory. The table was fine when we left, must have been burglars that broke in and smashed it up."

"Fit wye wid burglars break in jist tae vandalise a table?"

"Obviously we're gonnae have tae chore some stuff tae make it look convincin. C'moan tae fuck. His flatmates could be back any minute, like, have you thought ay that?"

The Mermaid nodded. "He's right, ken. We need tae get ootay here. Whit we gonnae take, Johnny?"

"Right, if we're gaun tae this perty, we could dae wi' some mair booze. Bobby, see what they've got, and mess the kitchen up while you're at it. Dave, you help yersel' tae the stereo and any albums you fancy. Mermaid, you dae the bedrooms. Pull aw the drawers oot, make it look for real but dinnae touch nothin wi' your bare hands. I'll get the TV."

"'Is is mental. I'm nae wantin nithin tae dae wi' it," Dave protested.

"Think ay it logically, Davie man. If it's a break-in the landlord gets the table sorted oot on the insurance. Same goes for anythin we take. If it's us he disnae get hee-haw and the Surfer's in deep shite. There's nae losers. We're kindae daein' awbody a favour."

"Careful ay dabs in here an' aw." the Mermaid cautioned.

"Disnae matter," the Monkey countered. "If it comes tae it, we've aw been in here kosher, like. C'moan, let's move it."

Out on the landing, he closed the door on the latch, which he broke with the third Kung Fu kick and they legged it down on to the street and stealthy up the side of Donaldson's Hospital until they found a skip brimful with builders' waste. Nobody heard them as the Monkey took the coat off, climbed in and buried the TV and hi-fi in the mock-Tudor moon shadows of the Deaf School.

They made their way in dour shamefaced silence through the West End and up round the back of the castle. Johnny attempted to lift Dave Bruce's spirits. "Will ye fuckin lighten up, ya big salad-dodger. Whit wis the alternative? Listen, I dinnae ken how much that table wis worth, but say it wis a thousand, any ay yiz got that kindae money tae spare, cos I ken I havenae, and ah'm guessin' the Surfer disnae either.

The Mermaid agreed. "Aye, c'moan. Is it a perty or a funeral we're gaun tae? Whit did you get, Bobby?"

He looked in his plastic bag as they turned on to the Royal Mile. "British cream sherry, Crabbie's, half a bottle ay Advocaat, a Mackeson and the airse end ay a rid Lambrusco."

Dave cheered up a bit. "It's like Christmas at ma grunny's."

Pausing only to spit on the Heart of Midlothian and to pass the time of night with John Knox, they descended the High Street. Bob wondered if the soor-pussed aul' Queen-botherer, a punter outspoken in his disapproval of graven images among a whole catalogue of other potentially entertaining shite, would have appreciated the irony of ending up as one himself. Down the Canongate they followed the sound of music up a close and a wee staircase. The flat was a Tardis, surprisingly spacious, loud and hoachin'. The first nasty shock was the presence of Shona, Carol and Richard. The second, for Bob at least, was that Morag McPherson was there. With Fucking Merchant Company Rugby Gorilla Simon. He went on a recce.

Dave Bruce, to his distress, was collared by Carol and Shona, both patently lagging. "You're one of Norrin's friends from last night, aren't you."

"Aye."

"I like your hat."

"Right... Thanks."

"Do you want some wine. Sorry, we haven't got any glasses. We're nurses."

"Please. That would be braw." He took the Blue Nun by the neck and took a healthy swallay.

"Is he not with you?"

"Who?"

"Norrin."

"No, em, we'd to take him hame... cos he wisnae feelin great, like."

"What's happened to your face? You need to get that cleaned and stitched"

"Och, it's, eh, nothin, like. Jist a wee altercation."

"With Norrin?"

"NO!... No, that's tae say, ken... He wis kindae involved, but it wisnae him that... and it wisnae me that...

"What? Again! God, is he OK?"

"Aye... aye, he'll be fine... in the mornin. Probably brand new, like."

"So, you've been in our flat again."

"Aye... That's correct..."

"You'd better not have left it in the state you did last night. The whole place stank. Crumbs and cans and greasy paper everywhere, your two friends in the nip on the sofa. It was disgusting..."

"Don't mind Shona. She's pathologically house-proud. She gave poor Norrin dog's abuse. At least you didn't scratch the table."

"Aye, when we left it wis... just great, like. Listen, will you excuse me, I've gottae go tae the lavvy."

"And we'd better go home and check on baby Norrin, Shona. Can we have our wine back?"

"Aye... of course... I... it's been fantastic tae meet you... we'll, eh, hopefully... I'll just..." Dave Bruce's legs malfunctioned and his nonchalant exit scored low on both technical merit and artistic interpretation. He joined the toilet queue and leant heavily hyperventilating against the wall.

The Waltzer Monkey set up court on the floor in a bedroom and sparked up. The sweet smell of the Stick attracted a familiar figure. The Man They Couldn't Hang clocked in and stretched out flat on the floor. "I am absolutely fucking spannered," he announced.

"Little Mermaid, meet Scouse Charlie, Scouse Charlie, meet the Little Mermaid." Charlie stretched out a languid hand which dropped to the floor as the Mermaid touched it. "Mmm... What dosage we talkin here, man?" the Monkey enquired as he exhaled a fragrant fog, his head went zero-G and his heart fluttered.

"I've 'ad three of the bastards."

The Mermaid was shocked. "We talkin aboot the same stuff we had last night?" Johnny Barr nodded. "Christ, you gonnae be OK?"

"Yeah, I'm sound, prin. Come 'ed, la, gis some of that bifter." Johnny inserted the spliff into the Moth's mouth like a periscope, and without the use of his hands, Scouse Charlie took a series of deep toots. There was no reaction to the burning ash that fell on his face.

By the time he got to the kitchen, it was evident to Bob that they'd arrived a bit late to be welcomed with brimming glasses of anything. Nothing but dead soldiers and demolished snacks. He scouted and rinsed out second-hand paper cups, and as he filled them, there, on the other side of the room, were Morag and Richard, in animated dialogue. On closer inspection, she was in tears. Even after all that had transpired, there was still something in that which upset him and made him want to make whatever it was better. Not the ideal circumstances, but he grabbed three cups and sidled over, blood thumping. He struggled to gauge how pished he was in relation to them, and to think of anything remotely apt to interrupt the evidently intense tete-a-tete. "Anybody for a sherry?" was as good as it got.

Richard turned to him as Morag turned away. "Oh hello, fancy seeing you here. Well, this *is* a charming surprise. I sometimes think I'm the only chap in the whole of Edinburgh who's that way inclined. And so novelly presented." As he accepted the crumpled offering Bob realised that the plastic bag between his feet was a grenade with the pin out and the heart rate went through the roof. "Is young Roberta with you?"

"Eh? Oh… no, he got really drunk, like. Had tae tak him hame."

"Really, you are a positively shocking influence on him. Normally such a sweet boy. Wouldn't say boo to a goose. Bottoms up!"

Bob took his first ever slug of sherry, emptying the cup in a oner. Fuck, rough as a wee hairy dug, but undoubtedly alcoholic. He swallowed hard. "Hi, Morag."

"Not now, Bobby, eh," and she was out of the room. He almost followed her.

Bob McMillan broke an awkward silence. "So how do you two know one another?"

"University. Any appearance of flippancy is deceptive, I too am a drab solicitor's trainee. You?"

"Aye. University too. Nae really my business, but is she OK, by the way?"

"Not especially this evening. Love her to bits, but God help her, she lurches from one emotional cul-de-sac to the next. All very entertaining, of course. One does have to watch absolutely every episode. She has an unerring knack of being attracted to beautiful shitbags." Bob took the compliment without acknowledgment. "Having said that, there was one chap, the Dark Lady of her Sonnets, as it were, if you understand my reference?"

"Do Cowdenbeath play attractive football? If you understand mine?"

"I have no idea. All shrouded in mystery, anyway. I never met him."

Suddenly the glamour crescendoed. The rest of the Roller Curry Girls helped Jane Cranston, her twisted ankle, broken heel and bruised arse out of a taxi, up the stairs and into the heart of the action. She spotted Morag and screamed. "Morag McPherson! Ya dirty Hielan' hooer!"

Morag forced a smile at the arrival of reinforcements. "Jane Cranston, ya slack Selkirk slut! What you done to yersel now?"

"Dinnae ask! Got rugby tackled at a roller disco." She looked over at a dead ringer for Plug from the Bash Street Kids who was slumped in an armchair nursing a can of Special Brew. "Hey, you, gorgeous, whit does a poor crippled lassie have to dae to get a seat in this cowp?" The homely youth rose unsteadily to his feet, advanced within inches of Jane, stared deep into her eyes, and summoned up the spirit of Sam and Dave, a sublime soul tenor warbling forth on a wave of halitosis.

As he came to the chorus, in slow motion, without losing eye contact, he rocked a couple of times, before pivoting backwards on his heels like a felled tree and evidently ending his participation in the evening's gaiety.

Jane's mates had made a pre-arranged stopover on the way from Coasters and come by no means empty-handed. They announced their intention to head for the kitchen to make tequila sunrises, and helped her into the chair. Morag sat on the arm, putting a brave face on it but betrayed by mascara.

"What's up wi' *you*, hun?"

"Ach, man trouble."

"Just the one this time?"

"Na, Doctor Jekyll *and* Mr. Hyde. I was out with him last night.

133

Top notch first date. Movies, Loon Fung…"

"Lemon chicken?"

"Do Cowdenbeath play attractive football?"

"Eh?"

"Just something stupid Bobby used to say. And then he chummed me home along the Water of Leith and there was just us and the moonlight, like, and we just got on so well, full fuckin Walt Disney, ken."

"Did you…?

"Not that it's any of your business, Miss Cranston, but no."

"Coffee?"

"Aye, but Heather and Jean were still up. Abernethy and MacFadzean are the self-appointed guardians of my morals."

"Fuck that! So you mean we're talking chaste kiss and offski?"

"Chasteish."

"Cor blimey, Mary Poppins!"

"And he's asked me to come and watch him play rugby this afternoon and we were going to meet up after but the bastard's stood me up and went out with his mates instead, and they've thought it would be a laugh to see how much electric soup they could neck as a dare and now he's showed up here and he's pished as an angry rat."

"Right, well, any of his nonsense and he's got me and the girls to deal with. Away and sort yer slap oot and we'll see you for cocktails in the kitchen."

Where a cottage industry was springing up. The ingredients were good to go, they'd even picked up the right glasses. The girls cleared the table and formed a production line.

Outside the lavvy Dave Bruce was aware of a figure to his right, who, to his relief, wasn't Shona or Carol or Richard. "It's Morag, eh? We met last night?"

"We did. How you doing, Dave? I like your hat, by the way."

"Thanks. You OK?"

"I'll be fine. Just need to sort my stupit face out. So do you, incidentally."

"Ach, it's jist a scratch. Wannae go in front ay me? I'm nae in a hurry, I'm jist escapin fae a situation, like."

"You and me both. How's Bobby?"

"Bittie pished, but still functionin.";

"I kindae cut him dead there. He must hate me."

"You appear tae be confusin him wi' a rational human bein. He's crazy aboot ye. Sad but true."

"Too crazy, but hey, the weird thing is there's not a day goes by when I don't kindae miss him. Are you happy?"

Dave looked surprised. "I wouldnae pit it quite 'at strong. My da used tae work doon in Wolverhampton. Used tae describe the English as simple, cheerful people. Dra' yer ain conclusions aboot fit 'at says aboot us Celts."

"See, I was. No ecstatic, like, but definitely happy. God, why am I telling you all this. I don't even know you. It's all fucked up, eh?"

The door of the bathroom opened. Dave jerked his head. "On ye go."

"Sure?" Dave nodded. "Come and have a drink with us in the kitchen, eh."

The Waltzer Monkey and the Little Mermaid came up for air from an epic French kiss. He reached over and extracted the spliff from the Moth's insensate lips and passed it to hers as two good-looking giants in expensive casualwear stumbled into the room, laughing like drains, sharing a bottle of Buckie. Memories may be beautiful, and yet, for Kelly at this point, they featured her father, whose relationship with the commotion lotion had become the defining factor in the life of the Reid household. She remembered how every evening, regular as clockwork, around nine o'clock the wreck-the-hoose juice would take over and the fear would descend. She was his favourite. It was a two-edged sword. Under less direct threat than her mother and wee brother, she was the only one who could stand in the way of the madness, any way she knew how.

"Hey, you, ya wee whore, is that a reefer?" was Simon's opening gambit, before he ripped it from her mouth, took a deep drag and coughed. "Look at us, we're hippies, eh? Peace, man." As he leant against a wardrobe and the rugby lads laughed inordinately at Simon's *bons mots* the Mermaid reached in her bag, got up and advanced slowly on him. He held the joint high above his head "Oh, you want it? Well, you'll have to ask nicely, won't you, dirty wee slag. What do you reckon, is your boyfriend man enough to get it back? Doesn't look like it, eh?" He looked over

136

at his mate. "Tell you what, suck my cock and I'll think about it."

To his pal, Simon was the King of Comedy tonight. He roared with laughter and put his hand up. "Me next, please!"

Simon didn't realise it was a familiar problem with a familiar solution. Down around his groin he heard the click of a spring-loaded mechanism and felt a sharp stabbing pain pinning him back. She looked up into his eyes. "Would you rather I didnae cut the devil's bagpipes aff? Well, you'll have tae ask nicely, won't you." He winced as she pushed the stiletto a little further forward.

Before Simon's mate realised what was going on, in one movement the Monkey was on his feet, picked up a bottle, smashed it against the window sill, and jammed the jaggy business end against his face yelling, "SOOK THIS, YA CUNT! Right, you, ya big walloper, whit's your name?"

"Simon."

"Nice tae meet you, Simon. Here's whit's gonnae happen. You're gonnae drap the bottle and give the Little Mermaid there her spliff back like a good boy or it looks like they'll be callin you Simone, eh? Whit about you, mate? Pardon ma manners. We havenae been introduced either."

"I'm Noah."

"You're kiddin me. After this we could call *you* 'No Eye', eh? And you know whit, you'd baith deserve it. You ken why? COS YOU'RE IGNORANT FUCKIN ENTITLED WASTES AY OXYGEN!"

Noah was shaking. "Fuck's sake, you're mental. Just let us go. We don't want any trouble."

"TOO FUCKIN RIGHT AH'M MENTAL! Whit dae you think, Kelly doll?"

"Up tae you, Johnny. Ah'm no bothered one way or anither."

The Monkey pressed the bottle gently into Noah's face and drew blood and tears. "Now then, Simon, you've been a clever boy so far. Next thing that happens is you get tae fuck wi' the understaunin that I will show you Noah's skull if you dinnae and if I ever see you again I *WILL* FUCKIN KILL YE, I swear I will." The Mermaid withdrew the knife enough for Simon to move and he jinked out the door. "Right, Noah mate, your job is tae make sure both ay youse cunts are ootay here when I come and check in five minutes. D'ye think you can manage that for me?"

"Yes."

"Oot ma sight, ya stupit fanny." Left alone, Johnny and Kelly held one another tight as the Moth began to snore like a pig.

Bob was enjoying the novelty of having a job. All he had to do was put bendy straws in the cocktails as the penultimate stage of the process before a hot wee black lassie called Toni applied the *coup de grace* with the umbrellas. His workmates were all bonny, the crack was hilarious, for the right money he could contemplate this as a long-term career choice.

The clerk of works, a willowy blonde known affectionately as Doonhamer Dolores called a smoke-o. "That's enough tae stun a herd ay moose," was her assessment of current productivity levels.

Back in control of the face, Morag clocked in. Bob grabbed a brace of glasses and sashayed over. "Crafted wi' my ain fair hands."

"Is there no *end* to the man's talent? Slainte. You're quite pished, eh."

"*Au contraire*. Just enough tae mak me wittier and mair attractive tae women. Here's tae crime."

"Tell me something exciting, then, Roberto."

But before he could Simon burst wild-eyed into the galley with Noah in tow, grabbed Morag by the forearm and made for the exit. "We're getting out of this dump!" was the only explanation he offered.

"Get your fucking hands off me right now! *We're* not going anywhere!"

Bob had got himself on the other side of them. "You heard her." And valiantly hurt his fist on Simon's chin. But that David and Goliath thing was just a lucky shot and an egregious piece of sensational journalism. The alpha male grabbed his opponent's shirt front with one hand and took out his frustrations on his face in a furious tonic-wine-fuelled frenzy with the other. The factory girls leapt to the aid of their workmate, cramping the huge No. 8's style a bit, but powerless to halt the carnage entirely.

Plug from the Bash Street Kids stuck his head round the door, retreated, and returned with a basket-hilted broadsword. He spoke in slurred, yet cut-glass accents. "Stand aside, ladies."

Simon paused the assault and turned to face the ill-favoured youth. "Who the fuck are you?"

"Since the recent sad demise of my dear father in the jungles of Borneo, I, young Lochinvar, am the fucking Earl of Caithness, and I'll thank you to get the cunting fuck out of my fucking flat." He advanced on Simon and as the other occupants of the kitchen cleared the piste, with his left hand on his hip executed a series of expert, if drunkenly dangerous sabre cuts around his adversary's head, a final flourish bringing the point of the weapon to rest against his Adam's apple.

Noah pulled Simon away. "Leave it, Si, he's not worth it," he advised, evidencing a weak grasp of the *realpolitik*. "Let's get out of here, it's too mental." Whirling in a maelstrom of incandescent rage, self-preservation in the presence of a stone-cold nutjob and loss of face Simon nonetheless did not resist, and they were gone.

Morag was the first to break the silence. "Emm… Thanks… Sorry to hear about your dad, by the way. What was he doing in Borneo?"

"We run a small orang-utan sanctuary. I'm going to bed now. Do enjoy the rest of the party." And he too was gone, his exit coinciding with Dave Bruce's entrance.

The big man surveyed the silent wallflowers. "Fit's 'e scoop?".

"Lang story, although kindae short 'n'a'. Suffice tae say, as you may notice, I hiv added my name tae the roll of honour entitled 'People who took an undeserved chinnin 'is wikkend.' Get yersel a fruit juice and hearken tae my tale ay woe."

The Mermaid and the Monkey floated in. "We're balin oot," he announced. Kelly led Dave over to Bobby and hugged them both together. She examined Bob's swelling puss and bleeding nose and shook her head. "Ah'm no even gonnae ask. Hope you Aiberdeen minks get some sex tae go wi' the violence."

Johnny Barr took over, bear-hugging the two lads. He turned to Dave and broke his hand again. "Fuckin gas tae make yer acquaintance, big yin. We've decided we're gonnae come and see yiz in Aberdeen. In the meantime, here's a wee something tae remember us by." He reached into the holy of holies of the criminal coat and produced a tiny square of blotting paper for each of them.

"Stick aroon, fuck's sake. Fit wye ye gonnae get hame this time on a Sunday mornin?"

"Krishna will provide. Far as this perty goes, the thrill has gone, but. We'll probably jist keep walkin west till we can hitch a ride. I could dae wi' the fresh air. So, Jane Cranston, Morag MacPherson, David Bruce, Robert McMillan, ladies, pals I've yet tae meet, hasta la vista and hope yer next shite's a hedgehog." And two more were gone.

She liked his hat... she was called Antonia Annan... she had been the only black kid in Kirriemuir... the first sook of the dayglo drink, he realised it was a bridge too far... and yet he persevered... he claimed he was a professional saxophonist... she was a total wee cracker... a medical student?... the white dress left just enough to the imagination... through thick Mexican goggles she must have mistaken him for a more attractive man... he couldn't recall either of them instigating it, just kindae happened... the first clinch must have been in the kitchen, there were cheers and applause... this much Dave remembered.

Morag MacPherson did not pause to admire the beauty of the sunrise. She necked three of them in quick succession sitting on the work surface in the company of her past and present hero, and it was like Mr. X and the Gorilla were written out of history. She'd never been a big drinker, and the tequila hit her like a goods train. When they'd been together, Bob had tried not to get too far ahead of her. He reflected that this was the first time they'd been properly pished together. That they should have done it before, this was a hoot. That it had always been the eyes. He hadn't met them all, of course, but it was inconceivable that there was a lassie anywhere who should even bother putting her name down for that competition. That making her smile was addictive, too much was never enough. That... just everything really.

"You do realise you look like a butcher's shop." Even this didn't break the spell. "Away and sort yersel out and I'll see you in the living room." He did and she was there with her coat and bag. "Come on and take me home."

She missed a step on the way down and he caught her but fell on his arse himself and they laughed as they emerged into the frosty early morning. A har was coming in off the Firth of Forth and mingled with their breath, the only sound in the sleeping city save the odd passing taxi. Above Waverley they stopped and looked down at the parked trains, still hours from their Sunday shift. He put his arm round her waist and they turned to face one another. He smiled. "Be gentle with me. Bittie tender aboot the chops, like."

Climbing the stairs at Doune Terrace they alternated between singing "Donald, Where's Your Troosers" and shooshing one other. Back in the day they used to lie in bed talking forever, but tonight Speedy Gonzalez was in a hurry and the clothes came off like in the movies. With an animal grunt he entered her lush pleasure garden.

"Party's over, big man." Someone was shaking Dave. He opened his eyes and looked around him. A few stragglers, and a great deal of debris remained in the room. He didn't recognise anyone. Looked at his watch. Five o'clock. Got unsteadily to his feet. A couple of girls giggled. Stumbled to the kitchen and took a long drink from the tap. Assessed the situation. Still aff his face, but nae aff his tits. He smiled to himself. That didn't even make any sense. A quick scan of the premises revealed no acquaintances and, most disappointing, no up-and-coming doctors from Kirriemuir. He was unsure if he was capable of making intelligent, or even intelligible conversation with strangers. An anonymous exit seemed like the way forward.

Down on the pavement he found himself enveloped in fog and silence. He could barely see the buildings on the other side of the way. Dave realised with some alarm that he had absolutely no idea where he was, and no means of navigation. He walked to the end of the road and found a street name. Bakehouse Close. None the wiser. Walking up to the top of the close he found himself on a wider thoroughfare, facing a church, and consoled himself with the thought that, if he hung about for a few hours, at least he was guaranteed that a congregation would show up who could tell him where he was. He put his hands in his pockets and stared at the church. And felt the blotting paper. He removed it and considered for a moment. He thought of his time at Sunday School as a kid, looked up again at the kirk, and thought of the black, joyless threats, the guilt trips, the knowledge that, waking up in the middle of the night, if he opened his eyes, Jesus would be standing there at the end of his bed, filled with disappointment at David Bruce's many misdemeanours and lies and at the warnings that had been ignored. Not a kid anymore, in the early morning fog, Dave whispered "Body of Satan" to himself and took his medicine.

He became aware that he wasn't alone. Two of Lothian and Borders finest had materialised from the mist on either side of him. Shite! Had they seen? He wasn't holding anything else, was he?

"You alright, son?"

"Ay, fine thanks, officer."

"If you're going down that way, you winnae get through. Palace gates are locked, like. Whit ye daein'?"

"Just on my wye hame fae a perty, like."

"Alright. You gonnae be OK?"

"Aye, I'll be fine"

"Behave yersel, eh." And they moved on before Dave thought to ask them where the fuck he was. But what he did now know was that there was a palace down the hill. Intrigued, he went to investigate. Buildings revealed themselves through the haze on either side until shadowy, beautifully-wrought pillared gates appeared before him. As they stopped his progress he strained his eyes through them and made out the vague bulk of a turreted fantasy about a hundred yards distant, spooky in the silence. He checked himself. No, didn't feel any different. This was real enough, but, shite man, happed in mist, the city that surrounded him had ceased to exist, and there was a kind of private Hammer Horror show going on for his sole benefit. This was brilliant. He should explore further.

The buildings thinned out, and he found himself in what appeared to be open country. At which point things started to go a bit funny. Kind of peculiar and ha-ha at the same time. Dave started to run. The streetlights in the fog were bright, blindingly bright, and *they* were coming towards *him*. At the speed of light and way out of control. He grabbed a piece of street furniture to stop the breakneck frenzy, spun round it, and sat on the pavement at the foot. He hardly dared look up. Slowly he turned to face the lamp-post. It was a very slinky lamp-post, bending and shimmying. Really sexy! And there at the top was Heaven. The light was unbearably bright, and yet he could see right through it. There were no things in Heaven, just flashing colours and stuff, but it was the greatest place.

Christ, he was beyond merely moist. Like, if a hundred people all threw a bucket of water over you, you'd be soaking, aye, but this was something else. It was the most refreshing thing. He was made of morning dew. He took his hat off, and it was made of dew too. No, not dew, silver, but then not silver, diamonds, millions and millions of tiny, impossibly sparkling diamonds. It was so fragile. He put it back on very, very carefully, got up, crossed the road and started walking across grassland. It was dark and exciting. His heart thumped like it was trying to escape. Soon there were trees. Not a forest, but a wee clump. With faces, obviously. They nodded for him to continue, and he did so. In the foggy dark, he stumbled into water. And there it was. Feet away from him. A white, white swan. It turned and swam away to his right and pointed with its neck. Dave disappeared again into the mist. Above him there was a ruin. He climbed and put his hands on the wet stones and they reacted, bending out of shape. Fantastic! He tried it again. How had he never realised he had these powers before? He vowed to use them for good. He could create the most beautiful things in the world, buildings, statues, sculptures. He would make the ruin into a cathedral. But not now. There were more adventures to be had. As he left the ancient monument he climbed again. It was important to keep going up. He heard his own breath like a rush of white noise. He made out what appeared to be a summit ahead of him, and then it happened. The cloud in which he walked lit up with a halo, a day-glo semi-circular rainbow above his head. He stopped in his tracks. It was the loveliest thing he had ever seen. It invited him in, and as he passed through the arch, it widened and suffused, and he emerged from the mist onto the top of a mountain, bathed in a dazzling light. He looked down, and the rainbow was spread out beneath his feet. The brilliance of the kaleidoscope on which he stood and which now started flashing and moving was too much to bear but too beautiful for him to take his eyes off. Dave stepped off the peak and walked down into the feathers of a peacock's tail. As he became totally immersed he stepped into nothingness, plunged through the void, landed with a sickening thud, and rolled. He scrabbled, desperate in the mist, at the rocks around him as his slide continued. He was aware of imminent, terrible, inevitable danger. Instinctively, in a frenzy, he kicked into the ground to get some kind of foothold. His foot hit a solid outcrop as his hand grabbed another. As he steadied himself his heart thundered. He looked out in the direction where the city should be.

In the cloud ahead of him, the face of a young girl appeared, twenty times life-size. Its eyes were fixed on him. The apparition was advancing hesitatingly towards him, sometimes seeming to cower down, and then rising up to reveal that it was carrying a scruffy rag doll, but always advancing, and never taking its eyes off him. As it approached, its size lessened, though still remaining far above human dimensions. Not fun any more.

Dave turned away, terror-stricken and the girl was there, on the hill just above him. Little girl-sized. She stretched out a hand and grabbed his. The slope was steep and she was tiny, and yet she pulled him, slow but steady, ever upwards, until he sat on a broad crag. She smiled and disappeared into the cloud. The hat was gone.

# 20

She woke him up. Took some doing. But he grinned realising where he was.

"What's the time?"

"About 9."

"Jesus. Go back to sleep."

"Can't. Been awake for ages."

"What you been doin?"

"Thinking."

"What about?"

"Us."

"And?"

"Not a clue. That's why I've been awake for ages. What about you?"

"What about me?"

"Tell me how you feel… about us. If that's something a bleak Aberdonian could have a shot at."

"Unconditional, I'm afraid."

"For real? Daft laddie. If I was you I don't think I'd ever speak to me again. Do you have to go?"

"What do you mean? I mean, no...och, but I'd have tae find Dave and tell him. He'll be expectin tae give me a lift up 'e road."

"Will I come up and see you in Aberdeen?"

"When?"

"Dunno. Soon"

"God! I need a minute here. I shall repair to the cludgy and contemplate your words. Can I bring you some tea back?"

"And toast, please."

"My pleasure."

"My stuff's third cupboard from the left."

Bob pulled on an exhibit from his Y-front museum. The uneasy stirring of his bowels led him to try a door. From her bed, Jean MacFadzean contemplated the bold figure with a semi standing backlit in the doorway. And screamed.

"Who are you? And what do you want?"

"Bit ay a sair heid. Hoo's yersel? As to my desires, I'd like world peace, an end to famine in Africa, I'd like to work with underprivileged children, and I'd really like the chance to do a bit more modellin. Also, I'm gaggin for a shite. Far's your shunky?... No... nae gonnae gie me a clue... never mind... it'll be an adventure, eh? Good talkin tae you."

Bob's next attempt was more successful... He sat down,

148

reflected on the strange but fortuitous turn of events and how much he wanted it to work out this time and turn his world downside up, be his salvation, and experienced the sinking feeling that life was never really like that and it was all too good to be true, before being distracted by the thought that even he didn't care for the reek he was producing. He consoled himself with the truism that something that evil was definitely better out than in. It took a couple of flushes and a hard shift with the brush to clear the bowl, if not the air. He exited to confront Heather Abernethy in Sunday best. Her expression told of the assault on her senses which the opening of the lavvy door had occasioned.

"I'd gie it five minutes, right enough."

"Are you Morag's friend? You made a terrible noise last night."

"Sorry, darlin. I was in passion's steamy grip, ken."

Miss Abernethy's face registered further distaste. "When you came in."

"Guilty again. Bittie pished, I fear."

Bob made his way through to the kitchen and set about preparing breakfast. All was going well until he was aware of the presence of MacFadzean and Abernethy in the doorway.

"Do you know that's my mug you're using?"

"No, but hum me the first few bars, I'll pick it up."

"Did Morag not tell you which mugs you could use?"

"Sadly she did not confide in me."

The toaster popped.

"Whose bread is that?"

"Dinnae ken, ask me one about sport."

"If you're using Jean's bread or my butter you must realise that it makes the whole system unworkable."

Bob trayed up the teas and toast and made for the door.

"Believe me, I do appreciate the potential consequences of my somewhat cavalier approach, but I take consolation in the fact that I dinna gie a monkey's fuck."

"Ladies."

# 21

The upside of being off your gourd on the top of a big old volcanic outcrop was that the geography of Midlothian was now evident. Still tripping a bit, Dave Bruce was readmitted to the North British Hotel by the same old, big, lavishly-white-whiskered doorman (He is the Walrus, Dave reflected) just in time for the arse end of breakfast. He ordered everything to which he was entitled and unnerved his fellow diners by his unbridled amusement at them, his breakfast, the entire situation, in fact.

Gradually the room thinned out until it was just him and a couple of waiters who were failing to see the funny side. And then swelled slightly with the arrival of the Cheshire Cat dressed as Bob McMillan. He flopped down in the seat opposite and helped himself to a tattie scone.

"Fit like, David?"

"Necked yon acid 'e Monkey gave us, so still a bittie spaced oot, since you ask. You try it?"

"Otherwise entertained, pal."

"So you and 'e lovely Morag…?"

Bob's stupid grin said it all. "C'm'ere, you gonnae be OK to drive?"

"I'll gie it a lash, like."

"I'll awa up and get my gear, 'en. Am I gonnae run intae Toni?"

"Na, made a bit ay an erse ay that situation, sadly."

# 22

A drive which should have taken three hours stretched into the dusk as Dave, ripped and sleep-deprived, crawled up the coast road. A cop car trailed them from Arbroath, shredding Dave's already fragile nerves. Just out of Montrose the blue lights and the siren came on, and as he felt his guts loosen the *gendarmerie* overtook *à toute vitesse*, the main event evidently now elsewhere. Appetite stopped the lads at Inverbervie for legendary fish suppers. Eating them overlooking the stormy beach, Dave spoke. "Cheers, Bobby".

"Think nithin o't, pal. Couldnae drive through Bervie and nae introduce you tae 'e delights."

"I didnae jist mean 'e fish, although you're right, 'is is pure quality, min. 'At wis some wikkend. Brillant tae get oot ay Aiberdeen. 'Ere's a big world oot there, eh?"

"Och aye. Top ay Denmark if ye kept on swimmin."

"Tell you fit, I'm nae gonnae spend 'e rest ay ma life sellin hearin aids."

They finally arrived back in the flat early evening. The only concession the bastard landlord had made to modernity was lit up like a Christmas tree. Bob pressed the play button. Roddy McMillan, the Silver Surfer and Johnny Barr, in that order. His Dad's stressed the urgency of a call back, but Bob decided to respond in reverse order of difficulty. 041, then.

"Pollokshaws Armadillo World and Tearooms."

"Monkey Man! Fit like? You get back OK?"

152

"Aye. Had tae hoof it tae Corstorphine, like. Goat a lift oaf a poax doactor."

"You get his number? Could come in handy."

"Cheeky cunt."

"Did 'e Little Mermaid get back tae Livvy?"

"Na, couldnae really ask the boy tae go oot his wye, like. Mermaid's here right noo wi' me and the wee scaly fuckers. You get back tae Sheep Central OK?"

"Aye. The big man had necked yon acid you gave us, so it was interestin."

"He's a fuckin inspiration tae us aw. Tell him tae get a fuckin grip fae me, eh. I tell you whit, I might hae a business trip tae the Granite Shitty next weekend. Ony chance ay a crash?"

"Mi casa, su casa n'at, Johnny, 'At'd be a gas"

"Lavish! Listen, probably see ya at the weekend, man. Gottae go, ah'm getting ma boaby sooked the noo."

No area code required for the next one.

"Where you been? I've been trying you a' weekend."

"I was doon in Edinburgh, Rodrigo. Fit's up?"

"Nae easy wye ay sayin this, son. Your ma's got cancer."

A feeling like his insides had been pulled out. Eventually. "How bad is it, Da?"

"It's her liver and her kidneys. They're sayin they've caught it pretty late. She's got an operation on Wednesday."

"D'ye want me tae come over?"

"Na, it's OK. Kathy's here wi' the bairns. But we're awa in tae Foresterhill tae see her the morn. I'll pick you up at 1.30, eh?"

"Aye, sure. Is there nithin I can dae?"

His voice breaking. "Nithin ony ay us can dae, son."

Bob sat on his bed, shivering. After a few minutes, Dave Bruce entered the living room and landed heavily in the armchair. "Ken 'is, I'm still a bittie trippy, min. Nae idea fit wye I managed tae get 'at car up 'e road. Cannae even mind much aboot it. Fit like yersel?"

"Ma mum's got cancer."

"Fit?"

"I cannae believe I didnae realise. She's got so thin and weak and tired and depressed. And I didnae think nithin o't. See wi' yer da. Fan did you think somethin' wis up?"

"Same as you, min. Kent somethin' wisnae right, but you think they're indestructible, eh? Even afore 'e divorce and him gan doon tae England I kent 'ere wis some kindae problem, but I suppose I jist pit it doon tae 'e domestic situation. Fan I think aboot it now, I think he mebbe kent himsel and runnin awa' wi' Sharon wis like a last throw ay 'e dice, ken."

"He lasted a whilie, though?"

"Och ay, they gave him three month and he lasted near three

year. He wis workin till 'e last couple ay wiks, so you're nivver sure. Fit're 'e docs sayin?"

"Dinnae really ken. She's an operation on Wednesday, though."

"Weel, listen, nithin you can dae except be there for her and get on wi' your life. 'At's fit she'd want, Bobby."

"Suppose. 'E Monkey's threatenin tae come up next wikkend. I'm gonnae ring him back and postpone."

"Na, like I say, life goes on, min. Even if you're nae in 'e humour, I'd like a couplae drinks wi' 'e gypsy king. You spik tae 'e Surfer an' a'?"

"Nae yet."

"Tricky, eh?"

"Jist a bittie. Dinnae think I'm up tae it 'e noo."

"Aye, except he's your mate and that's fit you need right now."

Fifteen minutes later and at a loss what to do with himself, Bob McMillan went for the 031.

An exaggerated Chinese accent. "Wes' En' Wontons. Wha' you wan'?"

"Is that Richard? It's Bob McMillan here. We met… this morning." It seemed a lifetime ago.

"Norrin's friend?"

"Aye"

"How are you?"

"Nae great, min. Jist found out my mother's got cancer." Why had he told him that? Barely knew him.

"I'm so sorry, Robert. Stay strong, brother. I'll get Norrin, will I?"

"Please."

"Bit complicated, we're not actually speaking to him right now. But I'll make an exception."

Voices in the background, then Norrin. "Chrehst, man, Richard jist telt meh about yer ma. How bad is it?"

"Disnae sound great, pal. I'll see her 'e morn. Fit like yersel, loon?"

"All a bit strehnge doon here. Eh wiz blehzin last neht, eh?"

"You most certainly were, kiddo."

"Aye well, I eventually got up this afternoon and it felt like somebody had behten the sheht oot ay meh."

"They did. Bouncer at Coasters Roller Disco, to be precise."

"Oh reht. Dinneh remember that bit. But it got worse. We'd got broken inteh during the neht. Hehl plehce wiz trashed, TV and stereho gone, lehk, and worst eh all, the tehble had got totalleh totalled. Armageddon, man! Landlord wants tae chuck ehs oot, Richard and the girls areneh spehkin tae meh, cos it occurred on meh watch lehk, but eh didneh even realise nothin wiz happenin. Apparentleh the polis interviewed me, canneh even mehnd that. Cut a lang storeh short, things are a bitteh tense

156

hehr. Eh wiz thinkin eh mehbe comin up and sehin you and the big man next wehkend, but wi' yer ma and everythin you probably dinneh rehlly…"

In spite of himself. "Na, c'moan up, Norrin mate. 'E Monkey's threatenin a visit an a'."

"Wi' the Mermaid?

"Mebbe. Dinnae ken."

OK. See ya Frehdeh neht. Whehr'll eh meht you?"

"Front bar at Ma Cameron's. Little Belmont Street, but ask onybody. Aboot ten minutes fae 'e station."

*Sotto voce.* "Shona's gehin meh the ehvils. Think sheh wants tae use the phone, lehk."

"OK. See you at 'e wikkend, min. Cheers, Norrin."

"Brilliant. Cheers, Bobby."

# 23

The next two days took on a grim routine. Roddy picked him up at lunchtime with Kathy and they made their way to Aberdeen Royal Infirmary. Mum's brave face failed to disguise the suffering or how scared she was. Conversation was forced, Mrs. McMillan didn't really have the energy for it. They would leave the room in turn to get a degree of relief. Bob couldn't believe how cheerful the cancer ward nurses were. Flirtatious, even. You found a way of dealing with it, he supposed, but, God, they were brilliant. The tea and biscuits just kept on coming.

For reasons best known to himself, Roddy announced that Bob and Kathy should spend some time with their Mum on their own. On the Monday evening, despite some trepidation, Bob went in by himself, and, right enough, that was a wee bit easier. He felt an unexpected sense of relief on his mother's part, like she didn't have to pretend any more. She could deal better with a duologue than a four-way conversation, or maybe, it occurred to him with treacherous guilt at even having the thought, a conversation that included his father. They had a laugh about how daft he was as a happy wee bairn. With what seemed to him unshakeable logic, he used to dry his teeth with a towel after brushing them. After all, you dried your hands after you washed them. He had expected approbation rather than derision. There were atypical and unaberdonian expressions of mutual love, and an unscientific assurance from Bob that everything was going to be OK.

Kathy and her kids took the next evening shift while Bob stayed with Roddy. He knocked up some mince, mealy puddin and tatties for his father, and they settled down to watch some shite on the telly. Conversation was, as ever, tricky. Eventually

Roddy spake thus. "I dinnae ken aboot you, son, but I could fairly dae wi' a drink"

"Nae bother, Da. Will I pour ye a dram?"

"Na, let's ging oot."

"Seriously?

"Aye."

"Far aboot?"

"I da ken. Far div you loons hing oot 'ese days?"

"A' sorts ay places. Ma's, Harriet, Lumpie, Prince."

"Prince ay Wales?"

"Aye."

"Christ, I hinnae been in 'ere for donkeys, Robert. C'moan, let's go. I'm buyin." This was most unanticipated. Especially the last bit.

Off the bus in Union Street and down the familiar steps again into the bowels of Aberdeen. For a Tuesday night the place was hoachin but no sooner had they crossed the threshold than a barman took their order over the top of the crowd. A pint of lager and a large Smith's Glenlivet in hands, they made their way to the back of the shop looking for a table, and there was Dave Bruce. Not solo, but, holy moly, in the company of Kim Anderson. He waved them over, and with some rearrangement of the furniture, they sat down.

"Fit like, Mr. McMillan? How's Margaret?"

"She's got her operation 'e morn, David, so she'll be fine efter 'at."

"'At's brilliant, Mr. McMillan. I'm Kim, by the wye. Dave wis tellin me aboot your wife. You OK?"

Roddy McMillan took Kim Anderson's hand and kissed it. What the fuck! Full of surprises tonight, Roddy. "Congratulations, David."

"Aye, weel, we're nae really... We jist got talkin oot on 'e street and... here we are."

Roddy downed his dram. "Fit we a' drinkin?"

With the old man up at the bar, it was Kim who asked the big question. "Fit's 'e real story?"

"D'a ken, Kim. Dinnae think she's gonnae be fine tomorrow, like, or next wik, or next month. Seems to me like she's pretty far gone."

She took his hand and squeezed it. "You never know, Bobby. It's amazin what they can dae 'ese days." This degree of intimacy with Kim Anderson would have been recently unthinkable. What the fuck was happening tonight?

"Far's Igor 'e night?" was the question that occurred to him.

"D'a ken. D'a care. 'At's so last wik."

Stop the presses once again. Dave's worldview underwent a *volte-face* and a universe of possibilities opened up. At the bar Roddy was in amused conversation with a barmaid. Bob clocked it. "Looks like time tae save a damsel in distress. D'a ken fit's got intae him 'e night."

And Mr. McMillan pressed on out of character for the rest of the evening, his wallet transformed from Fort Knox into Liberty Hall. The drinks kept on coming, especially for him, and with each visit to the bar he put the moves on a variety of inappropriately young women, and far from the cold shoulder Bob would have expected in his father's situation, the wit and repartee were going down a storm.

By ten o'clock they were all pished. Both Dave and Kim disappeared to the lavvy about the same time, and when Bob followed five minutes later, he was confronted with the prospect of his mate and the blonde bombshell in a meaningful clinch near the front entrance, as, he couldn't help noticing, a table of motorcycle enthusiasts looked on with surprise and disapproval.

Given what tomorrow held, Bob calculated that the evening's gaiety needed to end right about now. With some difficulty he extricated his father from the company of a pneumatic brunette and they jumped a cab in Back Wynd, witnessed by a recent arrival from the capital.

"You alright, Da?"

"Really, son? Hingin on by my fingernails. Dinnae trust 'at supercilious sleekit soothmooth surgeon. Fit like yersel?"

"I'm OK." He put his hand on his father's shoulder. "She's in 'e best hands, Da. Nithin we can dae except be there for her."

"I didnae deserve her, Robert. See Dave wi' yon lassie Kim. 'At's fit it wis like. I aye thought I'd lose her. I've been a very lucky loon."

# 24

The zookeeper's kindness had reminded her how stupid she'd been. Of course, she'd seen it on the TV, hitch-hiking was a thing, she didn't have to walk back to Aberdeen. She came down off the mountain on the Sunday morning, walked round a loch and out to the edge of the city. The wrong edge, as she was informed much later by the first person who stopped. Back in the centre her enquiries as to the whereabouts of Aberdeen were largely met with derision, or directions to the train or bus stations. Finally she found herself at the alternative of Turnhouse Airport. Maybe you could hitch-hike on planes? You couldn't. There weren't even any flights for Aberdeen on the departure boards. She asked about hi-jacking, but this was apparently not an option either, and brought with it the risks of further institutionalisation, and of pilots flatly refusing to be hi-jacked for such a short hop. As the cops hove into the mid-distance she vacated the airfield precincts and as dusk fell found herself in a lay-by beside the two biggest bridges in the world. Her one was nice, the other one was all rusty and manky. A huge lorry pulled in. Everything was big today. Hills, civil engineering, mistakes.

The driver said his name was Erchie. As an old hand at *noms de guerre*, she didn't buy it for a minute. You can't judge a book by looking at the cover… except there was something there that set old alarm bells ringing. Despite misgivings, though, he *was* going to Aberdeen, and she climbed in. It was warm and comfy. In Fife she added a massive yawn to the list.

"Tired, darlin? Aye, me too."

He pulled into a yard full of other lorries, revealed that he had a bed above the cab, and suggested that they should have a wee lie-down.

"OK. Is there a toilet as well?"

"Aye. Over there."

"I'll be right back."

In the dark she kept on walking past the toilet block into the woods. Scary, but not as scary as the alternative. Finally the trees thinned out and there were streetlights in the distance. And in a Dunfermline residential avenue, an unlocked shed with a bag of fertiliser as a pillow and sacks and a tarp as sheets. She slept well past the sunrise, walked into town and spent half of what she had left on a sausage roll and a bag of Revels before hitting the road again. Could hardly have gone smoother. Got a lift to Dundee with the Strongest Wumman in Kirkcaldy (official, she showed her the certificate) and on to Aberdeen with a children's entertainer named Uncle Jolly (neither entertaining nor jolly, as it turned out, but he got her there).

# 25

All too soon, Wednesday dawned. The op was scheduled for early afternoon, and ARI were running a tight ship that day. They had hardly arrived before surgeons, anaesthetists, nurses and porters started preparations. They held her hands till she was gone and they were ushered into a waiting room.

Roddy spoke first. "It's gonnae tak three oors, they reckon. Nithin tae dae here but wait. If you wannae get awa for a bit…"

"I'm stayin wi' you, Da." Kathy put her arm round him.

"Ken 'is, I might jist tak a stroll, if you dinnae mind. I'll be back." Bob rose, for some reason chose the inappropriate gesture of shaking his father's hand, and headed for the bus stop. Back in town, he spotted the tautological number 4 named "Sea Beach" and hopped on.

Coming down the steps from the prom, you arrive on a concrete landing with big slopes leading off to both left and right down on to the sand. Big enough to get a sizeable vehicle down, but you would first have to get it down the steps, which are narrow and, well, steps. Yet again, Bob reflected on the utter pishness of whatever crazed civil engineer had come up with this shite, and of the Corporation for giving it the green light. This pattern of steps, platform and slopes was repeated at regular intervals along the beach. Bob sat on the edge of the landing and put his feet up on the first upright of the wooden groyne which went all the way down the sand into the tide, high right now. Alone and sad as he watched the eternal waves, it still kind of felt like the right place to be.

As a bairn, the game had been to walk out as far as you could along the structure before it disappeared underwater. This was risky because the further out you got, the wetter, greener and skitier the wood became. If you got far enough out that you were above the sea, the worst that could happen was that you got soaking wet and bone-freezing cold, even at the height of summer. If you came off earlier it was a fair way down for a wee person, and your scrapes and bitter tears were guaranteed to elicit absolute zero parental sympathy, as the danger of the enterprise had, as they pointed out, been pointed out. How many times?

But his mum and dad weren't there. Slowly, carefully, one foot in front of the other, out he went. Just as scary as he remembered it. His foot slipped forward under him and he grabbed a stanchion behind to steady himself. His heart was thumping, for Christ's sake. He smiled through the tears that had started unannounced. Silly fucker! But he'd started, so... Onwards. The game he had just made up was that he wasn't going to turn back till his feet got wet. Over the water now, real slippy. He stopped and gazed at the sea, and time stood still. The breaking of the waves was hypnotic. He thought of his mum, memories, how she was now, how he could have been a different kind of son. The seventh was the big one. That's what they said. That one was quite wee. Keep goin, ya chicken! Don't even look. Till it's too late, and, sure enough, just as he did look, there it was. Number 7. Breaking just as it hit him, about knee-height. Somehow kept his balance long enough to flail out, twist and catch the wood behind him as he fell.

As he pulled himself back to his knees and looked down into the waves, he filled out a damage report form. Sore shoulder where he'd broken his fall, but that seemed like all he'd broken; big old stripe of smelly green slime all the way down him; wet from the waist down. Gazing back towards the safety of the beach, he noticed that his place on the arse end of the groyne had been usurped. An older gent. Unmistakeably of the alcoholic fraternity, and not of that chapter that still gets it together to go to board meetings. A jakie of the old school.

The tide seemed to have flowed quickly in whatever time had elapsed since his last visit to dry land, to the extent that his return trip could conceivably demand some cursory social interaction with his fellow beachcomber, just to get by him. As he made his cautious way back, Bob was seized with the unaccountable impression that he knew this chiel. There were certainly a few potential down-and-outs in his social circle, but none who had fully committed to the transition. His progress back was painstaking, and gave him time to rack his brains and come to the satisfying conclusion that this was in fact the very fellow he'd seen at the Castlegate, the man whose impromptu buffet had been interrupted by the ever-vigilant boys of Grampian Police, bored off their tits on a quiet Sunday afternoon. Coming closer, the extent of his new companion's problems came into sharp focus. The drink of choice today was a spray can of Bel-Air hair lacquer. Bob had never tried it, to be fair, even for its intended purpose, but he imagined that you would have to weigh the transient mule-like kick it would undoubtedly deliver against the loss of whole battalions of brain cells.

"Are you fae Atlantis, son?"

Unexpected, and worthy of a snappy comeback. "No man, my submarine's got a flat tyre."

"Hey, tell that fat cunt Poseidon tae get tae fuck."

Hmmm… a classical scholar, and yet… "'Scuse me, Jim, gottae get tae Kwik Fit before they close." And Bob hopped nimbly up on the concrete.

"Hey." He looked Bob straight in the eye.

"Aye."

"I loved her, ken? I loved her mair than that flash chancer Roddy."

Bob was mildly amused, being acquainted with only one Roddy. He imagined his father as the polar opposite of what he was, dressed in a stripey jazz-age zoot suit, snapping his fingers, drinking champagne, talking jive, and spending money on showgirls like it was going out of fashion.

Some way along the Esplanade he looked back and saw that the old jakie was walking away up the thinning strip of beach towards the Bridge of Don, and that he was no longer alone. A tiny girl held his hand as he remonstrated with her. She turned for a moment, not breaking her stride, and looked straight at Bob with sad eyes.

Back at ARI, there was no good news. The surgeon ushered them into a wee untidy office. It had been too risky to remove much of the tumours, and he was of the opinion that Mrs. McMillan was too weak to undergo therapy.

# 26

Back at the flat that night noise in the street woke Bob up. Bleary, he listened. Engines. Then footsteps on the stairs. An anonymous threat filled the air, like there was a poisonous snake sinuous under his duvet. Still he stayed in his bed. Subsequently somebody was chapping at the flat door. The curtains were closed, but he could tell it was the middle of the night. Who the fuck would be calling round now? He decided to ignore it, but heard Dave getting up. After that, it all happened very quickly. The front door opened, and he heard a girl's voice. He listened, alert now. Christ! That was Kim Anderson, if he wasn't mistaken, sounding upset, frightened, and then voices were raised. Lots of voices. People were piling in, and not in a good way. He heard Dave swear, then howl out in pain. Time passed, but he did not help his friend. Maybe it was a nightmare, but no, he was awake, wide awake. There were no words now, just kicks, blows, more cries of agony and a lassie greeting, and then the living room door opened and the big light blazed on. Dave Bruce was thrown into the room, a gaping wound stretching from his left temple to his jaw. Igor the biker, framed in the doorway, held an open razor. Behind him, another half dozen guys, in Nomads colours for the occasion. One held Kim by the hair, one held a petrol can.

"The wee cunt's here an' a'. Magic! Check it oot, he's keechin' himsel'. Thinks he's a smert cunt, this ane. Too much ay a shitin' wee hooer tae back yer mate up, though, eh? Tell you fit, 'is place is minkit. I thought you wouldae been mair houseproud than this, girls. You'd better gie it a wash, Fish."

The big, vacant-looking loon with the fuel can unscrewed the top and looked Bob straight in the eye, smiling, as he slowly began to tip the contents onto his bed, then the armchair and then the carpet.

"Fuck's sake, Igor, no!". Kim Anderson, screaming. He was on her in a split second, clamping his hand over her mouth and holding the razor to her face.

"Will ya shut it. It's the middle ay the fuckin night. Div ye want tae wake the neighbours up? Keep her quiet."

Igor gestured. "Gie't here."

He took the petrol and stood over Dave and Bob. Dave winced and roared as it ran through his hair and into the wound. As the last of the can was emptied over him, Bob sobbed and pleaded and the Nomads laughed.

The big biker produced a Zippo. He turned to Kim. "You can stay wi' yer wee mates here or you can ride wi' the boys. Up to you." The lanky lad who held her by the hair kept his other hand tight over her mouth. She shook her head as the mascara washed down her cheeks.

"Right, boys. Things to dae, people to see. When they ask you in Hell, tell them it was the Nomads."

He struck the lighter…

Nothing.

And again…

And again.

"Well, that's disappointin. Looks like it's your lucky night. A word oot o'your mooths tae the filth and it winnae be next time. Just nod if you understand. Good. You boys enjoy the rest of your evening."

They sat in silence till they heard the bikes disappear down the road. Bob had fetched a sweatshirt which was soaking up blood from Dave's face. He spoke first, his voice shaking.

"You OK, big man?"

"Been better, Bobby."

"I'm sorry I…"

"Dinnae be daft. It's nae your……

"Ay, but… OK, let's think… We've got to get you to Woolmanhill. That's nae gonnae heal all by itsel."

"I cannae go like this. They'll get the polis."

"Well, you cannae nae go. I've never telt you this before, but I'm shite at sewin." And an unforeseen aptitude for crisis management crashed to the surface. "Right, first thing we do is run you a bath. Wash 'at petrol aff as best you can and get changed. Then I'll sort masel' oot…"

"There's nae sense in you getting' involved in 'is, min…"

"Shut it, eh. I am involved. Then I'll take a bath as weel, cos, apart from anything else, I have actually keeched ma skids. Then we get ootay here, and we ring for an ambulance from a call box. Story is, unprovoked attack out on the street on the wye hame. Nae idea who or why. Unless you've got a better idea?"

Dave remained silent, shivering.

"OK, let's dae this."

Bob and Dave made their way down into the chilly night, turned on to Victoria Road and made their way down to the phone box. Ten minutes later they were on their way to hospital, Dave ashen and roaring as the ambulanceman cleaned the wound.

# 27

Sleepless after a night in Casualty they found themselves back at the flat. A frosty autumn day, but nothing for it but to open all the windows. The gas fire was obviously not an option. Dave's wound smarted like a bastard in the cold, and the petrol fumes made you dizzy and sick. As crisis manager, Bob phoned up Gogs's work. Must've dealt with a few petrol spills in his time.

"D'ye have cat litter? Or sawdust, but cat litter's 'e boy ideally."

"Fit wye wid we hiv cat litter, Gogs? I could try and get some, I suppose. How much do we need?

"Fuckin tons, by the sound ay it. Much as you can get yer mitts on. I'll come doon efter work and gie you a haun." As soon as he put the phone down, it rang again.

"Your ma's on her wye hame. Come ower."

"I'm a bit up tae ma neck in it 'e now, Da."

"It wisnae a question, Robert. We need you here."

Dave was given instructions to drive round Aberdeen and clear the city of cat litter. He dropped Bob off at the old McMillan place on the way, just as the ambulance arrived. Mrs. McMillan was wheeled in and hooked up to a drip. Bob hugged his sister and the kids.

"You stink ay petrol. Fit's 'e scoop?"

"Lang story, Kathy. Fit happens now?"

"Nurses'll be round every few hours tae check on 'e drugs. Apart fae 'at, nithin much, as far as I can see."

And indeed, Margaret McMillan slept through the afternoon and into the evening. Without going into too much detail, and very much against his father's wishes, Bob managed to make his excuses and escape, with a promise to return the next day.

Back in Torry, he was confronted by a scene of utter devastation. Gogs and Dave were adding the last bags to a thick grey layer of cat litter which covered his bed, and indeed the whole living room.

"So, fit dae we dae now?"

"Nithin. Just let it soak up 'e juice and 'e stink."

"How lang."

"D'a ken, Bobby. Owernight at least."

"Far am I gonnae sleep?"

"Dinnae ken, min. Ask me one aboot sport. My work here is done."

Bob made his way back to the ancestral home, where nothing had changed. He went straight to his old bed and slept for twelve hours solid. And still nothing had changed, except, Kathy said, their mother had taken a bad turn and at four o'clock a doctor had showed up with the night nurses and they upped the dose on the drip. She'd managed to have a bit of a conversation with her mum during the night, before the pain had got to be too much. Bob went through the house and held his Mum's hand as she slept for a bit, then spent some of the afternoon playing with his nephew and niece while Kathy dozed on the sofa, and, over in Torry, Dave Bruce disposed of cat litter as best he could.

# 28

The front bar at Ma Cameron's was small. Also crowded on an early Friday evening. Still, they could just meet up here and then move on. Bob needed somebody to show up, though. Right now he was out drinking alone with his guilt. He shouldn't be here. She was fading fast. This might be the night his Mum pegged it. The docs had let her home, the understanding being that they had done all they could, and that she might as well see out what time she had left whacked out on morphine in her own bed. It was horrible. There was no meaningful human contact any more, there was just sitting in that room waiting for the inevitable. Strangely, it was Roddy himself who had said he should go out, but he knew he should have refused. He just about convinced himself to put his pint down and head back home when there was a commotion at the door. A person was attempting an entrance and having his name taken in vain unanimously. "Fuck's sake, ye cannae come in here wi' 'at." "Ye've spilt ma pint, ya wee cunt!" Bad Vibrations as the end of a surfboard forced its way through the revellers followed much later by Norrin Radd.

"Fit the fuck?"

"There's a beach here, eh?"

"That much is true."

"Teckle. The hehl scehn in Embra's dead."

"Ain't no Surfin in Portybelly?"

"Precehseleh."

"Mebbe we should go ben the hoose. Mair room in 'e back bar, like."

"You no mehtin onybodeh else?"

"Waltzer Monkey's meant tae be showin right enough."

"With the Mermehd?"

"Didnae say."

"Whit aboot Dehve?"

"Hot date 'e night."

"If ah'd kent ah wid've brought ma ironin." The Little Mermaid made her entrance, looking hot in the Chinese jacket and skintight leather trousers.

"Where's Johnneh?"

"Dinnae ken. Takin care ay business. Said he'd see us later."

Igor only wore a suit for certain funerals. Business, however, was business, and the bouncer made no move to delay the big man's entrance into the wee doorway on the Adelphi. As advertised, his contact wore a long black leather coat. "It's in the backpack, big yin. Set ay scales in there if ya wannae check it." Igor removed the luggage from under the table and excused himself. On his return he pulled a bulging envelope from his inside pocket, sat down beside the Monkey and left it on the banquette. Under the table Johnny Barr ripped it open and did a quick count. £50 notes, right enough, and four of them were his. Easiest money he had ever made. He nodded at the big biker, they shook hands, and Igor was gone. The man who had followed the Monkey on to the Subway in Govan and the train at Queen Street rose from his seat at the bar, entered the gents and spoke into his radio, as the Monkey considered his options. He should be hooking up with the Surfer and Bob and the Mermaid right about now, but just needed a minute to calm the nerves. They'd have to wait for him. As he made his way up to the counter a hen party with the future bride angelic in white with an L-plate and her pals as lingerie devils piled in and joined him.

He turned to the nearest one. "You must be freezin. Can I get you girls something tae warm you up?"

Nine pina coladas and a pint of lager were ordered, delivered and swallayed not once but thrice before Johnny Barr found himself on the wee dance floor, the centrepiece of an erotic cabaret as Labelle sang "Lady Marmalade." The thought "I should be going" did occur to him, but the words never left his lips.

Under instruction from the bar staff, the surfboard was manoeuvred from the front snug to the spacious back bar of Ma Cameron's, accompanied by appropriately stirring sounds from the fiddle, squeezebox and bodhran ensemble which had sprung up in the corner. Bob vowed to keep coming through and checking for the Monkey's arrival, but after a couple of drinks they reasoned that he would check through the house if he didn't find them first off, and interest waned from the Surfer in particular, confronted as he now was with the perceived opportunity to get in the Mermaid's underclothes. Eventually it was Bob who suggested moving on and after some tricky negotiation, they managed to leave the board in the cloakroom at Fusion and made their way to the dancefloor, but it was wall-to-wall cheesy disco and his heart wasn't in it. He should be at his parents' place, but he couldn't leave his guests on their own in a strange city, not that they appeared to care. The Mermaid and the Surfer were cutting a surprisingly impressive rug out on the floor and oblivious to his very existence as he drank warm beer in a corner. Scunner! Which was interrupted by the advent of Ferret in a Travolta suit with much of the Innes pigeon chest on show and gigantic shirt collar worn outside the jacket and a bottle of Moet and glasses. He poured one for Bob and freshened his own up. "Fit like, min?"

"Ye see it a', Christopher. Fit like yersel?"

"Livin 'e dream, Robert. Tell you fit, pal, pished aff wi' yer big mate. Fucker hisnae showed up for work a' wik, and 'en, 'e night, I hid tae pit in an appearance at a perty tae ile 'e wheels ay commerce, like, and he's there, but get 'is, nae solo, he's wi' Kim fuckin Anderson."

"In a meaninful wye?"

"Sookin 'e coupon aff her, like."

"Aye, 'at seems tae be a developin scenario in 'is big village, right enough."

"Jammy fucker! But in 'e meantime 'e hale hearin aid business is on hold. Sales opportunities are bein missed right, left and centre, min. Job's yours if ye wint it."

Bob considered this for a nanosecond. Christopher Innes's proposal introduced a much-needed element of clarity to his scrambled heid. He listed the things he didn't want to do.

1. Sell hearing aids for Ferret.
2. Spend another minute in this shite nightclub.
3. Hit his own knob with a hammer while drinking bleach.
4. No, that was it.

178

He herded the Surfer and the Mermaid off the floor, picked up the board and they headed down past the station, along the end of the harbour, across the bridge and up the hill. On arrival, the Ansaphone flashing was the only light in the place. There was no doubt in Bob's mind that it would tell him that his mother was dead. No sense putting it off. He pressed PLAY.

"Aye, Bobby, dinnae think I'll be hame 'e night, so if onybody wants tae use 'e East Wing.... Probably see you 'e morn, min. Hope yer ma's OK... Cheers."

Dave had done good work. There was still an imperceptible grey layer covering the front room and a residual reek of fuel, but, on the plus side, the long-standing gollach infestation no longer seemed to be a thing.

Back at his flat, Igor heaved some of the contents out of the backpack. Not being a user he had no needle, but a hankering to see what all the fuss was about. He skinned a generous pinch of the Chinese White and sparked up. Almost immediately, his shite week was forgotten in a wave of euphoria. Fuckin Kim could fuck right aff, she never made him feel like this.

He considered his options. While it was tempting to do fuck all, a synthesis of sensations seemed in order. The only other thing that made him feel this good was the bike. He changed and made his way down on to the street. As he kicked the Z1000 into action and made it roar, two Panda cars rounded the corner. He pulled out and they followed. Not the kind of ride he had been hoping for, but if the fuckers wanted a race... A ton down Holburn Street, he had never felt so alive, through red lights, across the old bridge and a sharp right on to the South Deeside Road. Blue lights and sirens behind him now. Fair play to them, he hadn't lost them yet, but he could really open up now. As he approached the Maryculter Bridge he could hear them in the distance but he was out of sight. If he'd made the decision to recross to the north side of the river a fraction earlier... but he struggled to hold the wobble as he took the hard right turn way too fast, a car's headlights confronted him, the Kawasaki hit the parapet and he was flying through space, looking down at the rocks of the River Dee and flailing. The blue light intensified as more emergency service vehicles joined the scene. Somewhere off Rosemount, Dave and Kim turned the noise of the party into a background track as they climbed the stairs, their breathing becoming the dominant motif. The door he opened featured a bed strewn with coats and he hesitated, worried that someone might disturb them retrieving one of the garments, but she entered the room and took his hand.

Much later Bob was vaguely aware of the door opening. The Little Mermaid stood by his bed. "Shift ower."

"Eh?"

"Ah'm horny."

"I'm kindae spoken for, and fit aboot 'e Surfer, or 'e Monkey, is it?"

"Dinnae ken whit happened tae Johnny, and ah cannae wake the Surfer up."

"You're full ay surprises, Little Mermaid."

"You've gottae watch every episode right enough. C'moan, ah'm very good at this. Ye winnae regret it." Kelly Reid was wearing a Dundee United shirt, which she removed. As it turned out, she was only wearing a Dundee United shirt. She pulled the covers back to reveal that everyone in the room was naked and slid in, as, a little later, did Robert McMillan. The Mermaid had not oversold herself. It was one of the dirtiest and consequently briefest experiences of Bob's young life. He apologised, she replied "Isn't nature wonderful?", kitted up again and returned to Dave's room, and a further layer of guilt was added to Robert's already highly culpable existence. He lay awake and resolved to rise early and go and see his mum.

# 29

'But mousie. Thou are no thy-lane

In proving foresight may be vain.'

Once more the roar of an engine awoke him. Bleary, he registered the alarm clock. 10am. Shite! Unsteady to the window and, Holy Fuck, there was Morag MacPherson disembarking a wee Italian sports car. Looked new. He struggled to conceive of a world in which he would ever have that sort of money and despair piled on top of self-loathing. The bell rang, sounds of footsteps on the stairs. Bob opened the flat door as she arrived on the landing and ushered her through to the living room, as the Little Mermaid came out of the bedroom, wished them a good morning and headed for the lavvy.

In a stylish *ensuite* in the West End of Aberdeen, the Monkey awoke surrounded by women in various states of *déshabille*. Including the betrothed, he noticed. He hadn't, had he? On reflection, actually, oh yes, he had. This seemed like the very moment to slip away unnoticed. He fished a crumpled piece of paper from the depths of the coat, finally managed to hail a passing cab on Queen's Road, and it was only then that he thought to check, but aye, after a few moments of pure back seat terror, the fat envelope was still there. The taxi pulled out, followed by the Ford Granada which had been waiting outside all night.

Morag in the bedsitting room. Everything seemed back to normal to Bob, but she was shocked. "Christ. What's happened here?" And he made them a coffee and brought her up to speed regarding life's varied vicissitudes, leaving out the precise details of his previous night's adventures. A quick visit to Mr.

Aziz, and the smell of breakfast brought forth the grinning Surfer and the Mermaid. Rather than endure the toxic atmosphere of the living room, Morag squeezed them all into the kitchen, and given the ingredients and equipment to hand and the potential threat to life that using the electric rings posed, she put together a perfectly acceptable fry-up.

"Whit'll we dae?"

Bob was torn. The advent of Morag McInphrequently changed everything. "Dinnae ken, Little Mermaid. I should ging and see ma Ma. Ma heid's mince, though. Mebbe we should go for a wee walk first, like, blaw awa the cobwebs, ken."

The exit from the flat was observed from behind a privet hedge across the road. As the ragged procession featuring a silver surfboard snaked along the foot of the harbour, a taxi pulled up and the Waltzer Monkey joined the promenade.

"Where'd *you* get tae, then?"

"Takin care ay business, doll."

"How'd it go?"

"Smooth. Morag, this is a charmin surprise, by the way! Whit's a girl like you daein in a fishy dump like this?"

"I think I'm going to the beach. No really the weather for it though, eh?

"Not at all, it'll be fehn once wehr in."

"You're pure on your own there, Jim."

"Whit's up, man? Can you no swim or somethin? Eh can swim

lehk a fuckin barracuda, meh."

The Surfer had been struggling with a dilemma. As they passed the fuel tanks at the end of the docks, he elected to adopt the bold approach and turned to the Little Mermaid. "Eh've written you a poem. It's called 'Kahuna'.

"Ka-whit-noo?"

"Kahuna. Heh's lehk the god eh surfin… Feh Haweheh."

"Well?"

"Whit"

"Dinnae staun there lookin glaikit. Dae the poem"

"Eh dinneh ken if eh should now."

"Fuckin spit it oot, will ye"

"OK. Hehr goes. Kahuna."

> "Teh worship Kahuna
> Under the moon, a
> Glistening curve
> Of foaming surf
> Cools meh brehn
>
> The ocean's past
> It cannot last
> The wehves are now
> Theh show meh how
> Nothin remehns
>
> The future's beach

Within meh reach
It draws me on
And on the sand
Eh hold your hand
And then you're gone"

"Is that it?"

Norrin ignored the barely suppressed hilarity behind them.
"Aye."

"Poetry's shite, eh?

"Thanks."

"I mean, in general. I kindae liked your poem. Whit wiz it
aboot?"

"Surfin and girls."

"Will you write it oot for me?"

"Do you rehlly want meh to?"

"Aye. I've never had a poem."

"OK."

"So d'ye think this boy Kahuna's really like God?"

"Aye, well, eh suppose so. But heh's no lehk a big geh wi' a
wheht behrd. It's just lehk a fehlin you get from everything
around you. Ye ken lehk when things mehk you smehl."

"I think it must be brilliant bein God. Cos he gets tae kindae
organise his ain big soap opera. When he gets bored wi' people

he can just kill them aff. Like "Dallas", ken. I used tae watch that aw the time when I wis inside."

"Insehd whehr?"

"Inside… the hoose. We didnae hae an ootside telly."

*Déja vu* for Bob as they made their way through Footdee and to the end of the sand. The beach strangely deserted on a Saturday morning. It was fucking freezing, to be fair, but you might have expected the odd dog walker.

A few hundred yards down the shore, Norrin put the surfboard down and stripped off to a pair of bulging string-sided Y-fronts through which luxuriant tangerine pubes poked. Morag had never seen such hairiness in a youth. If push came to shove, she reflected, there was a place in Borneo where he could probably be happy.

Even the Monkey was taken aback. "Christ! Is Fred Astaire in there an' aw?"

"I'll tell you what he has got in there. You wouldnae think so tae look at him, but he's hung like a fuckin hoarse."

"Little Mermaid, are there any guys on this beach you havenae pumped?"

She looked up and down the sand. "No right noo."

Turning visibly azure, flattered and shocked in equal measure by the Mermaid's words, Norrin picked up the board, walked straight into the waves and paddled out, shrinking the equine appendage to more manageable proportions. The wind was whipping up a violent swell. He contemplated graceful exit strategies.

"D'ye think he's really gonnae?…

"I think he's gonnae die. How caul must that be?"

"I'm freezing right here right now, I'm gonnae head back."

"I'll come wi' you, Morag."

"I'd prefer a minute to myself, Bobby."

"OK, is this aboot fit 'e Mermaid said, cos…"

"I'd be a bit of a hypocrite if it was, eh?"

"Right. Tak 'e keys. I'll see you back at 'e flat."

"No, I'm gonnae head back to Edinburgh. This was a bad idea."

"No it wisnae. Dinnae go!" But she already had.

The Surfer paddled out to the point where the wooden groyne submerged then swam, tugging the board, to the structure itself, climbing up and returning to the shore along it, walking his surfboard behind him.

"Well, that wiz a desperate fuckin anticlimax, so it wiz."

Through teeth chattering like a wind-up joke-shop toy, "I ken the conditions look good oot thehr, Johnneh, but wi' the weh the tehd's flowin, there's a rip could tehk you clehn oot teh seh. Theh meht fehnd your board, but you wid be fish food."

"Have you no even got a towel, ya daft wee shite?

At which point a squad car and an unmarked vehicle screeched to a halt on the esplanade. Brian Bruce and a uniform colleague piled out of the former, two members of Strathclyde DS the latter. As they came down on to the strand they eyed the shivering Surfer, his ginger hairiness, his overall blueness and the board with extreme suspicion, but, unable off the top of their heads to think of anything strictly illegal to charge him with, they made straight for Johnny Barr, restrained him roughly, informed him they were detaining him under the Misuse of Drugs Act and went through the coat.

"Fit 'e fuck ye daein, Brian?"

"Stay oot ay 'is, Bobby. Trust me, ye dinnae wint tae get involved. You're playin wi' 'e big boys noo."

The envelope was fished out and inspected, the Monkey was read his rights in the matter of the supply of a proscribed substance, cuffed and helped up the steps to the waiting vehicles. Before things got totally out of hand, Bob made the call that this was the moment to finally head for the old McMillan place. The Mermaid announced her decision to leave her natural habitat and return to Livingston, and Norrin was given the flat keys and directions to Grampian Police, Queen Street to check on the Monkey.

In Torry, the Yale lock presented no difficulties. All the while she was in the flat searching, the phone rang repeatedly and almost incessantly.

Every way Bob turned, fires were raging out of control, but he prioritised and stuck to his guns. Coming down the familiar street of his childhood, the first thing he noticed was the Morrices from across the road, decked out in red and white, heading for Pittodrie, and then the unfamiliar big black car. As he got closer, the McMillan front door opened and Kathy came out, followed by the men in black with the zip-up bag. He ran the rest of the way, and hugged her on the doorstep.

In a voice free of emotion, "Where were you, Bobby?"

His father joined the scene. "Da, I'm sorry, I..." Roddy walked straight past him and had a brief conversation with the undertakers before they drove off.

# 30

Monday morning at the McMillans'. She waited until they had all gone out to the lawyer's. The back door was easy. Hardly worth having a lock on it. Knowing where to start was harder, but it had to be here. She had been through Bobby's flat with the proverbial fine-tooth comb.

In the parental bedroom, having gone through a chest of drawers, instinct led her to the wardrobe. She carefully removed some old photo albums, memorising how to put them back exactly as they were, and below them and an old newspaper, there it was. Thank Christ, Seamus had been in a foul mood ever since he'd found out it was missing. As he drank, he progressed from maudlin to raj on the subject. Despite the fact that the McMillans might be back any minute, she took the time to read the front-page story and study the picture, and in putting two and two together became the only person not directly involved to make four. She reflected that she was wasted outside the CID. The cruellest thing they had done was to deny her access to books as a punishment, but she had stolen the story of the Christ-like Lion and the White Witch and, on the off-chance, pushed aside the dresses and coats. No way through to the Winter Kingdom, but a painting of two youths, who she correctly identified as early incarnations of Roderick McMillan and George Fraser. It looked like a ragged old theatre poster she had seen in Edinburgh. She covered her tracks and slipped out leaving no trace.

# 31

Bob's maternal grandfather had been a Church of Scotland minister, who, you got the impression, had never quite come round to the idea of Roddy as a son-in-law, or even his ma as a daughter, come to that. A fierce and scary hellfire and damnation man of the old school of copious eyebrow, nose and ear hair who even had the reek of sulphur about him, in Robert's recollection. As a wee boy he remembered going to a wedding at which he officiated. The groom had been married previously, and the Reverend had devoted the first ten minutes to the topic of adultery, which Bob had taken as the state of being grown-up, although it had been drummed into his ungrown-up brain that thou shalt not commit it, so how did that work? After his grandfather's death his parents had gradually stopped going to church on a Sunday, but Kathy and Bobby still went to Sunday School, with a bribe of sweetie money to spend at the paper shoppie opposite the kirk. One day Bob had knocked on his parents' bedroom door and been admitted to find them in bed, quite the thing with coffee, rolls and the Sunday papers.

"Do I have to go to Sunday School?"

"Do you not like it?"

"No, I really, really hate it."

"Well you shouldn't go, then."

Simple as that. Kathy had gone by herself that day and was outraged to find that non-attendance was an option.

That had been the end of the family's involvement with the vengeful and smitey God so in vogue from the Solway Firth to

Unst from the Reformation to the 70s.

And yet when it came to his ma's funeral old habits died hard. They pitched up at the auld kirk on a bleak dark-grey day that other places imitate but only Aberdeen can truly deliver. In the graveyard a pit and stone lay ready. "It's what she wanted."

The new minister was considerably less confrontational than the old model. Certainly not remotely clappy or even happy, but seemed to have got wind of the New Testament somewhere along the line. He spoke of Mrs. McMillan's long-standing relationship with the church, but otherwise seemed to have done little homework and mouthed platitudes from the General Assembly of the Church of Scotland's "What to Say if You're in a Bit of a Hurry to Get Home for your Tea" playbook.

Uncle Dod, Mrs. McMillan's big brother and Roddy's best mate from way back when they were teenagers was much better value with the eulogy. No great biographical detail, but some cracking old stories of Bob's parents. He worked the crowd like a stand-up. Smiles and even some laughs through the tears. The mood lightened somewhat, and Bob couldn't help noticing some unsuitably older men eyeing his twin, smart as a whippet in black and unaccompanied except for her kids, with a priapic speculation.

As he carried his Mum out into the rain with Dod and a couple of undertaker's monkeys, Bob noticed three faces poking over the top of the kirkyard dyke. Two human, the larger one holding the smaller up to get a good look and one stitched roughly together. The wee girl, seemingly distraught, lifted the doll's arm and it waved goodbye. The hairy old beachcomber also wept. "What the fuck!" Bob stumbled and almost lost the coffin.

As they walked from the grave Dave came alongside. "Did you see 'e wee lassie?" Bob nodded. "It was her, eh?"

"Aye."

"Too fuckin' weird. I think I seen her in Edinburgh."

"In Embra?"

"Ay, up Arthur's Seat, I think. I wiz trippin aff ma tits at 'e time, so I'm probably nae 'e maist reliable witness."

"How's it gaun wi' Kim?"

"Amazin, min. She wis gonnae come 'e day. But she felt she'd be intrudin, like. She's awa tae see Igor in 'e hospital instead.

"Nothin trivial, I hope."

"Quite 'e reverse. He's came aff his bike ower 'e side ay 'e Maryculter Bridge. Totally smashed up and his heid was under water fan 'ey found him. They think 'e bike's probably landed on him for guid measure. A vegetable for 'e rest ay his natural is 'e prognosis."

"Mebbe 'ere is a god. How's 'e hearin aid business, by the way?"

"Ower and done wi'. Me and Gogs are awa tae see aboot roustabout jobs on 'e rigs 'e morn."

"You sure, min? Fuckin roch aul' life, 'at."

"Money's fuckin amazin, though. And two weeks on 'en two weeks non-stop perty, like."

"You comin back tae 'e hoose for a drink?"

"Said I'd pick Kim up fae 'e hospital, min. Is 'e Surfer still at 'e flat."

"Ay, but he can crash on my flair. It's your room, Christ's sake."

"Fit aboot 'e Mermaid?"

"Awa back tae Livvy."

"I'll probably jist stay at Kim's."

"Gottae say, it's a gey attractive alternative. If you're sure?

"Ay. I'll see you soon." And he was off.

# 32

"Bide wi' your Granda, kids. I'm just gonnae have a chat to your Uncle Bobby."

Kathy and Bob walked out into the weather in the wee back garden where they'd once played. Hadn't seemed small then.

"Christ, Kathy, it's pishin' it doon. We'll catch wir deaths." He saw she was crying. "Sorry, that was a stupit thing tae..."

"Shut up, please, Bobby." He put his arm round her. She wriggled away and lit a cigarette. Eventually. "Did you speak to her?"

"Aye.... Sure. We spoke. Before she was so out of it on the morphine at the end, ken."

"But did you really speak to her?"

"Aye. You were there a lot of the time, Kathy."

"But when you were on your own with Mum. What did you talk about?"

"Ach, old stuff, ken. When we were wee." He took his hanky out. "You've got me started now."

"Did she talk to you about when she was young?"

"No. Nae really."

"She did to me." She stubbed out her fag and walked to the back door. She held the handle and leaned on it.

"And.......?"

"And she made me swear."

"Swear what?"

"I cannae betray her, Bobby. I promised." She lit another cig and turned to him. "Promised I'd never tell you. And I cannae tell Dad. And I'm not strong enough to live with it all by myself either." She walked down to the vegetable patch and stood in the rain. "Fuck's sake, say something, will ye."

Bob was at her side. "I dinnae ken fit tae say, Kathy. If it's something you don't want to tell me.... Come in oot the rain, will you."

"Of course I want to tell you, but maybe nae today, eh. You probably ken some ay it already."

"Like?"

"You ken she went tae art school, aye?"

"Fit? Oor ma? At art school? Dinnae think so, Kathy."

"True. There's a portrait somewhere that she did of Da and her brither. That's how they met. She left a' that behind her efter... Oh, Christ, I wish I hadnae said anythin. Just forget it, alright. She was right. There's nae need for you to know any ay this. Just forget it."

Back inside, Bob made himself useful filling glasses, then, at a loose end and out of small talk, he went up to his parents' bedroom. Just Roddy's bedroom now. He opened the wardrobe. His mum's clothes. A pellucid, gauzy summer dress that he had never seen, nor could imagine her wearing. For the first time that day he really cried. Proper floods. He sunk to his knees, and, at the bottom of the wardrobe, there they were. The old photo albums. For some reason, it seemed like a logical thing to take them downstairs. He removed them, and underneath was a random old sepia copy of the *Press and Journal*. "BEACH TRIP ENDS IN TRAGEDY". He took the photos downstairs and laid them on the dresser in the sitting room, went and poured himself a whisky, and on his return, Kathy and his Uncle George had beaten him to it, and had an album of old black-and-white shots open. A snap of their mother as a vivacious teenager with a killer smile, at the carney with candy floss. Kathy had got her looks, Bob had got Roddy's. Scunner! "Will we get Da over."

"Na, Kathy, he's nae dealin' wi' 'is too weel. Might tip him ower the cliff, like."

"He's fairly hittin the sauce right enough." Another photo. George and their father unexpectedly with extravagant quiffs, sports jackets and rolled-up jeans. "Christ, Dod, is that you? Fit a honey! Fit happened? You'd some heid ay hair!"

"I hid it fan I needed it, Kathy."

They leafed through their parents' marriage album. Eventually, a snap of their Ma, stunning on her wedding day yet with faraway eyes, and a stranger, yet not quite a stranger, as it seemed to Bob. "Fa's 'at?"

"Let me see now." George put on his specs. "Oh aye, I actually took 'at photo."

"Did they nae hae a photographer?"

"Aye, that wis him. Said he always hid one photie ay him in amang the shots. Like Alfred Hitchcock, I suppose."

He looks kindae familiar. Fit wis his name?

"If I ivver kent, I cannae mind noo, Bobby. Dis it maitter?"

George went over and joined Roddy on the sofa. They exchanged a few words and his father looked over at Robert with what appeared to be loathing.

Kathy had moved on. She called her kids over. "Liam, Alice, c'm'ere! Here's me and your Uncle Bobby when we were wee."

Kathy leafed through the album, which was organised chronologically backwards. From Bob's graduation to Kathy's wedding to school clothes and sports kits to nappies on the beach to wee faces in prams. One of which she didn't recognise. "That's nae you, Bobby, is it?"

"Na, dinnae think so. Dinnae think we ivver got solo shots, did we? Difficult tae tell at 'at age, but 'at's a wee lassie, is it nae?"

"Ay, ye'd say. It's definitely nae me, though. How come she maks 'e cut?"

"Nae idea. Mystery cousin?"

"Na. Unless…"

"Fit?"

"Nithin." Kathy closed the album decisively. "I think Roddy's hid enough. Pairty's over, eh?"

# 33

Bob stayed that night but excused himself in the morning to go and see how Norrin was getting on. The news was not good. "Your landlord showed up last neht. He was mad as a fuckin cut snehk about the cat litter and the petrol and that and he ehven said you wereneh allowed teh heh surfboards. Whit a cunt! Eh explehned everythin, but he wasneh hehin it. Chucked meh oot but eh had the kehs. Wants you and Dehve oot, though, beh the wehkend. Says he's gonneh sue you for the cost eh getting the plehce gutted and rehdecorehted. And the Monkeh's remanded in custodeh in Barlinneh, beh the weh. Dehlin skag, theh're sehin. Could beh lookin at a lang stretch."

"Apart fae that, Mrs. Lincoln, how did you enjoy the play?"

"Sorreh, man, you dinneh nehd this on top eh yer ma, eh? I should go, eh?"

"Far wid ye go?"

"Embra, Dundeh. Dinneh ken."

"Stick aroon, pal. I could use a mate right noo."

"You've got Dehve."

"Dinnae even ken fan I'll see him again. He's wi' Kim and I dinnae hae a number or an address for her. Onywey, I think he's oot on 'e rig ony day noo. Listen, I'd better heid back tae ma Da's. I'll be back roon 'e morn's morn. Fit ye gonnae dae wi' yersel?"

Norrin shrugged. "Probableh go surfin lehter."

"Ken 'is, you need yer heid examined, ya raj."

"Och aye. Young and mental. If you've never caught a wehve, you will never understand."

Back at the parental home it was evident that Bob was unforgiven, but Kathy insisted they put on a show of normality for the sake of the kids. Late in the afternoon everyone but him piled into Roddy's car and headed for the shops to get something for tea. Left to his own devices, Bob wandered ostracised, lost, desperate and aimless about the once-happy house of his boyhood. The photo albums were still out on the sideboard, and he leafed idly through them again, collected them up and returned them to the bedroom. And there was the old newspaper. August 1968. The front page story was about the drowning of a bairn, swept away by a wave on Aberdeen beach while engaged in the risky pursuit of groyne-walking. Kirsty Mitchell. From Perth. The only connection the family had with Perth were his Mum's Uncle and Auntie, now long deceased. Why had they kept this? He unfolded the paper, and, near the foot of the front page, there was the photo. A wee girl with a doll.

# 34

The next few weeks saw Bob and Dave's eviction though not their prosecution come to pass and the Silver Surfer's mysterious disappearance. Dave wasn't too bothered. He now had the job on the rigs and had done his first couple of hitches, so was only spending half his life on *terra firma* anyway. This, together with his unexpected good fortune on the Kim Anderson front, and everything in the Bruce garden was lovely. Bob, meanwhile, moved his stuff back into the old McMillan place. In the car on the way there he filled Roddy in on the broad details of the Nomads' attack on the flat and lied about its role in his absence at the time of his Mum's death. His father didn't seem to believe a word of it, and the relationship remained chilly. Kathy went back to Peterhead with the kids, and Bob tried to balance being there for his Dad with avoiding the toxic ambience which now prevailed. Conversation was limited.

"So, fit ye gonnae dae noo, loon?"

"Hivnae got a clue, Da."

He was out most nights though he was now skint and found himself in the grip of a deep despair.

# 35

"You're Bobby's pal, eh?"

"Aye, who are you?"

"You can call me Uglina."

"Uglehna!"

"Aye, and this is Seamus. He's a bittie pished. Werenae plannin on sleepin here, were you?"

"Aye, well, it's out eh the wind."

"That's why we sleep here. Fit's 'at?"

"It's a surfboard."

"Like in Hawaii Five-0? Why?"

"Cos eh'm a surfer. Theh call me the Silver Surfer."

"How's Bobby daein?"

"No greht. His ma's dead."

"We ken."

"You deh? How?"

"I'm observant."

"And heh's got evicted feh his flat. Eh was stehin thehr as well.

That's wheh eh'm here. Eh'd get oot, but I've no got eneh moneh left and you canneh rehlly hitch-hehk wi' a surfboard."

But Uglina had excused herself and cleared off into the gale which howled like a soul in pain around their shelter. Seamus spoke. "Just leave the surfboard. Get out while you can. I would if I could."

"Eh canneh lehve the board. Surfin's meh lehf. What's stopping you, Seamus?"

"I'm too set in my ways to start again somewhere else. We all mythologise ourselves, I ken, but I'm used to it here, I know where to get a drink. I should think I'll die here. Maybe we all will. I cannae see a way out for any of us. We're too stupid to do anything about it, eh? I cannae even look after Kirsty any more. I used to have money coming in for that, but that's stopped now."

"Who's Kirsty?"

"Lassie that was just here."

"Eh thought she was crehed Uglehna."

"She's really Alison, I think. Disnae matter anyway. You're probably not really called the Silver Surfer."

Torchlight illuminated them. PC Bruce approached. "Aye, Jimmy, nae planning ony arson 'e night, I hope."

"I was fuckin freezin, Brian. Wasnae me that started it in any case, by the way."

"Ay, that'll be right. Fa's yer wee pal?"

"This is the Silver Surfer, Constable."

"Haud on, I ken you. You were there when we arrested yon dealer fae Glesca, eh? Didnae recognise you wi' yer claes on. Assume the position, Sonny Jim." Norrin was comprehensively frisked, but, much to the chagrin of the big polis, nothing illicit was forthcoming. "I've got my eye on baith ay yiz," was his parting shot.

The wee lassie returned. "Is that him awa?"

"Aye, how come you kent heh wis hehr?"

"I telt you. I'm observant. We'll let you stay if you get us something to eat."

"Lehk eh said, I dinneh heh neh moneh. Starvin masel, lehk."

"Christ, this is fuckin useless. What we gonnae dae?"

"Nae need for foul language, Kirsty. We'll set fire to a bin and see what tomorrow brings." He took a healthy slug from a nondescript blue bottle.

"I cannae dae this ony mair. What's the point to our lives? What am I doin here wi' you two losers. You're both aff yer heids." And she was gone again.

"A trifle harsh, didn't you think, Silver Surfer?"

"Will she be OK, do you reckon?

"Och aye, she's a survivor."

"Somebody once said that about meh. Eh'm no seh sure oneh mehr."

# 36

It was nine o'clock on a Thursday morning, down by the harbour, when Bobby realised he had to escape. He had spent the night on his pal Fraser Cattanach's sofa. Christ, he wasn't even really his pal, they just happened to have gone to school together and happened to have both been in the Blue Lamp at closing time. Catty had bought him a couple of drinks and said to come back to his flat for a beer, and he lived with this lassie Sarah now and she had been in a foul mood and they'd had a big argument about him staying and Bob had half-heartedly said he'd go, but it was pishing with rain by that time and he'd ended up on the couch and they both worked and they were up early and they'd offered him a coffee, but you could have cut the atmosphere with a knife so he made his excuses and left.

He crossed the road to the station and looked at the departures. Next train to leave was for King's Cross in five minutes.

On the journey south he jinked between toilets, heart like a jackhammer, avoiding the ticket mannie. Having got away with some half-arsed excuse as he passed him somewhere around Montrose, he was confronted once again as he exited a lavvy.

"You got your ticket on you this time, son?" Big Geordie, ex-military, probably, Bob thought.

"I'm sorry, back at my seat again."

"Fine, we'll go and have a look, will we."

And the train came to a halt. Bob glanced out the window. "God, is that Dundee already! My stop." He pushed past a wee family and their luggage and, resisting the temptation to break into a mad guilty run, did his best purposeful walk down the platform, looking with a grave concern at his watch, as if this was somehow proof that he was a very busy young man whose failure to carry his ticket with him when moving about the locomotive could be excused by his preoccupation with the important meetings he had on Tayside that day. Not having changed his clothes or washed or shaved for the best part of a week, any neutral observer would have dismissed this scenario as bollocks. The adrenalin flowed, but the noisy pursuit never materialised. Bob watched from the ticket hall as the last carriage pulled out, full of dreams of Leuchars, Inverkeithing and Darlington.

A train for Waverley arrived, and this time he found himself a cludgy and just stayed in it all the way. Somewhere in Fife the door handle rattled, and, after a few minutes, a battering on the door.

He heard a voice, "Christ, I think somebody's died in there!" and an answering laugh, and then a muttered "Fuck's sake" and then nothing. Gone to find another lavvy. Or to get the guard? A day with the British Transport Police seemed bang on the cairds. The sound of the train changed and through the wee non-frosted spot on the window there was every painter's Sisyphean nightmare, the old Forth Bridge. OK, not very far now. Just off the bridge the train stopped. South Queensferry. Unbefuckinlievable! Just fucking get on wi' it! Who gives a fuck about South fuckin Queensbastardferry! A nervous wreck by Haymarket, then the train seemed to slow to a crawl. He could visualise the castle. Were they passing it yet? Not at this bleeding rate. Perversely, after all this time, he really needed to take a shite right now. They stopped again. A voice:

"We'll be arriving shortly at Edinburgh Waverley, the terminus of this train. We're held at a red signal, should be on the move in a minute."

No sooner were his breeks round his ankles and a waterfall of runny shite on its way down the pan than the train lurched forward and hurtled in to the platform. He heard voices, passengers disembarking, then it went quiet.

This was obviously the time to skedaddle. Mission accomplished. And yet Robert McMillan found himself detained by a worrisome question of moral philosophy. The sign on the wall was unequivocal:

PLEASE DO NOT FLUSH TOILET WHILE TRAIN IS IN STATION

Bob could absolutely see the logic. There you were, bidding farewell to a loved one, perhaps not knowing when, or if, you would ever see them again. Tears, and one last kiss, and a wave of the old hanky as you lost sight of them and the train pulled out of the station, and as the last carriage passed you, there it would be, a fresh pile of steaming turds to sit alongside the memories of the first kiss, the laughter, the secret smiles, the tears, the sunny days you thought would never end. And yet. Some poor, underpaid British Rail cleaner was very soon to be faced with the toxic mixture of squittery keech and Izal which he now contemplated. Fuck's sake, Bobby. Get a grip. If in doubt, do nothing. Get aff the fucking train before something else happens. He opened the toilet door and there stood the very cleaner in question. With a mumbled "Sorry", he jinked by her and jumped down on to the platform.

At the ticket gate, a huge fierce-looking British Rail wifie, who eyed his descent from the train with a wild surmise. A mere ten yards away from her, two coppers in amused conversation with another BR employee. Shite! He stood transfixed. The only plan that came to him was to leg it, along the length of the platform, down onto the tracks and back towards Haymarket. A Mexican stand-off. At which point the gadge who was with the polis went for his radio. The BR man spoke to his colleague.

"Isa, need you on platform 8. Inverness train's comin in, they're saying there's naebody there."

"Aye, but…" She pointed at Bob.

"Any time now, Isa. Chop chop Chrissake."

Isa gave Bob the evils, gutted at a confrontation with Joe Public missed, but waddled off into the crowds. The mannie likewise gave the cops a quick "See ya later" and disappeared in the direction of the Travel Centre. Deep breath. Like you own the place, Bobby. The brace of filth watched as he passed. Nonchalant stroll. Don't look back. You will turn into a pillar of salt. Or the accused.

Up on Princes Street, he found himself once more outside the North British Hotel. He leant on the wall by the entrance. Drained in every sense, he looked up at the doorman, raising his hat to a well-heeled-looking old couple as they entered. Same guy. Jesus, that was another country.

A grey windy day in the capital. He watched the people hurry by, hunched against the weather, and the heartbeat reverted, in time, to normal. When he got on the King's Cross train back in Aberdeen, he knew all along, deep down, that he wasn't going any further than Edinburgh. He had to see her. It was half past twelve. Walking up to St. Andrew Square, in another nod to the past, he found himself outside the Café Royal. Would this go better with a drink inside him? He pulled a handful of change from his pocket. Na, dinnae be daft, how would that help? Turning along Queen Street, he checked the brass plates. Very soon, there it was. Vincent, Sprott, Provan and Kelty, W.S., dirty-grey, austere yet unmistakeably opulent. Serious white people. Bob felt under-everythinged, a ragged, useless mink. He went down into the Gardens, found a bench and watched and waited. What would he actually say? If it didn't feel right, he didn't have to do anything. And he'd have come all this way for nothing. Get a fuckin grip, Robert. One o'clock passed. And one-fifteen. Maybe she'd gone for an early lunch. Maybe there was another entrance round the back. Christ, this was hopeless. He was actually shaking.

He looked back up and there she was on the steps, but not alone. They were laughing about something, and Simon put his arm round her and kissed her. Fuck, this was not how it went in the movie. Bob turned his back and wished himself invisible until he got his head round this latest development. Ignoring earlier good practice, he looked back, and their eyes met. She pointed, and it was already too late. Here they came.

Simon spoke first. "Bobby, my man, how you doing?" Like he was his best pal or something, when in fact their previous social interaction had mainly involved the fucker holding the front of his collar with his left hand while he pummelled his face with the right. "We were just talking about you the other night, wondering what you were up to. Where are you working? Still up in Aberdeen, or are you down here now? I tell you what, sugar, I'm going to get a sandwich, I'll let you two catch up. Good to see you again, Bobby." He gave her another lingering kiss and he was off, turning to wave as he went.

The first thing to say was that Morag McPherson looked like a million dollars. The hair and make-up were immaculate. Charcoal grey two-piece, white blouse, high heels, black... they would be stockings rather than tights. Bob allowed himself a futile horny moment imagining the lingerie ensemble. Also, he was no jeweller, but the earrings, the necklace. He threw it out there.

209

"Goodness, what lovely diamonds."

Terrible Mae West impersonation, but quick as a flash: "Goodness had nothing to do with it." And they both smiled, and for a second it was all OK. "Listen, I'm freezin my tits off here, let's get inside somewhere? You look terrible, by the way."

In Henderson's, they sat by the window. In a classic Aberdonian gambit, Bob had suggested they go somewhere less expensive, prompting Morag to offer to pick up the tab, in the interests of getting out of the wind right now. Face was saved, and Bob was stuffing *his* stupid face like a big stupid horse.

"Hungry?"

"I'm absolutely ravishing. You still in the flat with the gruesome twosome?"

"No."

"I didnae think that would last, right enough. Fit happened?"

"Did you not read about it in the papers?"

"Since when did your domestic arrangements become news? You didnae lose patience and kill them, did you?"

"Did it all by themselves."

"Eh?"

"It was a Sunday. When I got up they weren't around. I didnae think much of it, just thought they'd gone to church. Simon was back at his parents' place, and I wasnae feeling great, so I just had a lazy day, watched the TV. Got to the evening and there was still no sign of them. I went and looked in Jean's room, and the bed hadn't been slept in, and that was weird because she'd been there the night before. I'd actually gone to bed before them, cos I was feeling a bit rough, wiped-out like, ken. And then I looked in Heather's room, and they were there."

"What had they been doin all day?"

"Christ, have you no been listening, Bobby? They were in bed, in one another's arms."

"What....like?

"Naked... Deid. Half-drunk bottle of champagne and two glasses on the bedside table. They didn't drink. And a box of chocolates and a bottle of pills. They'd left a note. They said sorry to everybody. Jesus and the Church of Scotland in general and several specific ministers, the University of Edinburgh, their parents, their teachers, the Girl Guides, fuck's sake. You name it."

"Christ, Morag... If they were that sorry for toppin themsels, why did they nae just not dae it?"

"They weren't so much sorry for the suicide; they were sorry for being in love with one another. They said they had chosen that night to express it, physically, like, but they realised that what they were doing was sinful, that they couldn't expect all these people they were apologising to to accept it, but that they couldnae live without one another, and they knew they were going to Hell and they deserved it. Fucked up, eh?"

"Aye. God, hey, I didn't really know them, but the one time I did meet them I'm afraid I was a bit of an arse."

"They did mention it."

"So what happened? You know, after…"

"Police, forensics, Procurator Fiscal's guys, journalists, it was a fucking circus. Then there was a Fatal Accident Inquiry, which was just horrible. Heather's parents own the flat, and I couldn't stay on there by myself anyway, so I was a bit stuck, but Simon was living with his parents at that point and they were brilliant, they took me in, and we've just moved into our own place in Marchmont last weekend… He's a good guy, Bobby. You'd like him if you got to know him."

"Disagree strongly. Tick."

"OK. Dead-end conversation. To be fair, you were both pished as wee beetles…"

And they chatted through the rest of her lunch hour, and smiled and laughed and he never wanted it to end, but he knew it already had. Outside the window a few wind-blown flakes intro-ed the first snow of the year. She looked at her watch. "Shite, Bobby, I've got to get back."

And then it all happened far too fast. She waved the waiter over and paid him, and then they were out on Hanover Street, and she was late. They kissed and he held her like he'd never let her go. He knew that when he did she was leaving for another world that he'd never be a part of. "Keep in touch, Bobby", she said, but it was just a thing you say to people you meet on holiday. He watched her disappear up the hill. At the top she turned and waved, and disappeared round the corner. Maybe there were tears. She was too far away for him to tell.

A beautiful red setter approached him, tail wagging, thought better of it, and hunkered down on the pavement. A man with a lead walked past and whistled. The dog followed him, leaving a fresh pile of steaming turds.

Curiosity led him all the way down Princes Street, through the West End, and along Haymarket Terrace. No response at number 84. He was just about to continue his walk west with a view to hitching back home when there was some noise from behind the door. Carol, in pyjamas and dressing gown.

"What do you want?"

"You dinnae mind me, eh? It's Bobby, Norrin's mate, fae Aiberdeen. We met the ither weekend."

"Sorry. Oh aye. *That* weekend. I'm still half asleep. I'm on nights just now.

"Christ, sorry to disturb you. You seen the Surfer?"

"Thought he was with you."

"Na, hinnae seen him for ages. Mebbe he's gone tae Dundee."

"I phoned his parents. He's not with them."

"Really?"

"Aye, I was worried, and now I've got them worried too. Most of the time he's fine, but he's got a crazy streak."

"He does."

"I think he might do something really stupid. This is shite. I really miss him."

"I thought you guys werenae gettin on."

"You cannae stay mad wi' him. Shona tries, but it's my wee Norrin we're talking about here. I want him back, and no just cos he's ridiculously well-endowed, to be frank. He's my best pal too."

"So you two are?… I didnae ken."

"Aye. Sometimes. We dinnae really advertise it."

With the change in his pocket, Bob got a bus out to Gogarburn Mental Hospital. Maybe a few days as their guest would do him good. His heid was certainly splattered all over the carriageway, but he got the sense that it wasn't the sort of place you just checked out of when you felt like it. He had some experience of the institute, having played fitba there once, press-ganged after waking up on the floor at a party into playing in goal against the staff. His net had been surrounded by the residents, who showed him no mercy. He stuck his thumb out and was taken to Forfar by an ames taper (something to do with plasterboard), to Laurencekirk by an artificial inseminator (pig wanker) and to Aberdeen by a colonic irrigationist (who failed to sell the concept of his services to Robert). All these things he could be doing with his life to make an honest buck, and yet…

# 37

Eh'm on the beach. Wi' ma board. The thing wi' surfin is, if you want to get good, you've got to go out evereh deh. No excuses. Eh meant to go earlier todeh. The weather wisneh so bad then. To tell you the truth, eh prefer goin efter dark, though. It's kindeh magic, and you dinneh get mehneh noseh bastards watchin you. Surf's up toneht, reht enough. Gonneh beh a chilleh one. When eh'm paddlin out, eh get acclehmatehsed teh the conditions queht fast. You'd think that was the borin bit, but eh love it, man. Eh'm at pehce wi' the ocean, and ma mehnd just wanders whehrever it wants to go.

The Policeman's notebook: Claes on the beach. Now that's just annoying. I mean, it could be a clue, but it could be a clue to just about anything. And that's the end of my shift. Life's too short.

Fuck, that wind's getting up. Bit scareh now. Na, it's gonneh be brilliant. No fear, eh'm a surfer and eh dinneh geh a fuck. Best surf eh've ever been oot in.

"246 to control. Over."

"That you lowsed, 246? Over."

"Aye. Spik tae you 'e morn…Out.

OK, Bobbeh, this is it. Big one comin. Eh'm gonnae ride it all the way to the behch and then call it a neht. You're gonneh be fehn, man. You can do this. Up weh go. Here it comes. Now or never. Shite, man, that wind is fehrce! Losing meh fuckin balance…. A massive silver craft passing over the water at low altitude. Canneh worry about that the noo.

215

"246 to control. Over."

"You getting overtime for this, 246? Over.

"Tell you fit, probably nithin, like, but can ye hae a word wi 'e Coastguard for me, eh?"

Weh dehp underwater now. Lehk a cormorant. Get teh the surface. Get teh the board. Eh'm trying teh get teh it, man, but eh cannae see it eneh mehr. Chrehst, eh'm a long weh out. Those lehts on the esplanade, they're fuckin mehles aweh. Eh'm surprised the carneh's still open. Theh'll be closin soon. Very cold. When the wind dehs doon you can still hehr the music.

A vision of a gravestone flashed into his mind:

## ROBERT LORIMER
### 1958–79
### HE HAD A HUGE PENIS

Survival superceded a search for the silver surfboard as he swam for the shore. When he checked, he had made no progress. Just tiring himself out. Been as productive going in the opposite direction and holding out for Scandinavia. Might as well tread water and conserve energy. "This is it, then. Whehr it all ends." He thought of all the stuff the people he loved would have to sort out. Realised that he loved people. As time passed, colder and weaker. Not as scary as you'd think, though, actually. Kind of like an uncomfortable dream. Nothing he could do about it, nothing anybody could do. Confused now, breathing slow, shivering, trying not to swallow and inhale too much seawater, drifting away for who knows how long. Three tiny lights in his imagination. One green, one red, and then a little higher, a white one. They disappeared. Definitely losing it now. But reappeared. And then, all of a

216

sudden, as he slipped in and out of consciousness, a big white light blinded him. Corny, is this really how it ends? Indistinct voices across the waves.

# 38

Scotland slept soundly, for the most part. In Torry, Mr. Aziz, insomniac for as long as he could remember, worried about the shop. He couldn't keep going forever. The dream had always been that Zayn would take over, but that was not the path he had chosen to follow, and no-one else in the Aberdeen Muslim community had a son who was a doctor.

In West Lothian, Mr. Reid was equally wakeful. A stubborn infection had set in, the pain was constant, and stronger analgesia had not done the trick. His daughter had no such problems. In the circumstances, she couldn't go back to the family home any more, had visited Johnny in the Bar-L, and it was arranged that she should take over his room in the Pollokshaws flat until the trial at least. Her new housemate tightened her tourniquet and made the syringe spit. In other clinical news, Ian Gordon, though unable to communicate, was vaguely aware of the night nurse feeding him and changing the colostomy bag, and Dr. Ibrahim, the new young Peterhead GP, wondered how it had come to this. He would marry Amal next May, and yet, with Liam and Alice at their father's place tonight, he lay, in direct contravention of his oath and faith, in Kathy's contentedly sleeping arms.

In another bedroom in Marchmont, after frankly fantastic sex, Simon produced a small velvet box which he opened to reveal a sparkle in the streetlamp coming through the gap in the curtains.

The Monkey got on well with his cellmate, but there could be no question that auld Shuggy Docherty was dangerously insane. He was up in court next week for, he claimed, simply doing his job as a school crossing guard. It eventually transpired that he had been naked at the time of his arrest, and in possession of an axe. A disorderly orgasmic commotion woke Johnny up and the

218

screws entered and attempted to restrain Mr. D, whose costume and prop of choice tonight were a crushed strawberry velour bra and panties and a huge manky lime green dildo with which he fought them off.

Comfy and cosy in his dream, Roddy danced better than he ever had in real life, slipping and a-sliding light as a feather with Maggie as Little Richard hollered and hammered his piano.

A matter of life and death, the casualty was transferred quickly to the ambulance before any evidence could be gathered, and PC Bruce bade his farewells to the crews and walked home through the howling windy litter-strewn night, watched by a young man working late through the picture window of his top-floor plush new harbourside office. Ferret had the catering contracts now for a dozen oil rigs and counting. Having no background in that industry, a huge slice of bluff had been called for, but it had been swallowed hook, line and sinker. He had done his sums cannily and the profit margin was astronomical, his shrewd investments had increased exponentially in value, and he reckoned he was two phone calls away from control of the helicopters that serviced the platforms. He fixed himself another coffee, put his feet up on the desk, watched the rain hammer the window and a tiny girl passing by through it and thought impure thoughts of Kim Anderson, who lay awake missing Dave. When he was home, the town was theirs, and got painted a very bright shade of red, in between trips to Edinburgh, Glasgow, and lately, London, Paris and Milan. She supervised his new wardrobe and he had already shed a stone. When he was offshore, she was a lassie from a cooncil hoose in Sandilands Drive suffering from impostor syndrome.

Uglina had witnessed everything, running as fast as her wee legs could carry her to the boathouse at Footdee. Now she walked unhurried across town to the McMillans' place.

Jean-Baptiste no longer worked at the airport. What his old colleagues never knew was that he was a tightrope walker in his spare time. Now, despite having no visible means of support aside from his rope, he gathered like-minded fearless individuals from across the Midi around him. An accountant who could juggle anything, the more dangerous the better, down-and-outs who breathed fire, a fisherman who did motorcycle stunts, even genuine circus clowns who embraced his vision of revolution. The first show was on Saturday in Montpellier. The public would not know what had fucking hit them. He dreamt that she would be there. After all this time, he still couldn't get the Scottish redhead he had once met out of his mind.

# 39

And then, out of the delirious incubus of his icy demise, a familiar voice. "I think 'at's him comin roon, nurse." Looking up at fluorescent lights. Lying in clean crisp white sheets in pyjamas that were not his own. Hooked up to all sorts of shite. Feeling like he'd been hit by a train, but warm, although it was snowing outside the window. A Christmas tree and decorations. Crazy! How did he get *here*?

"Hiya, Robert, you're a very lucky boy, ken 'at? Cup ay tea?"

Weakly. "Aye, please."

"Sugar?"

"Loads."

"Anither one for you, Robert 2?"

"Aye, go on, 'en."

"How am eh dehin?"

"Weel, you're nae deid. You'll be in here a whilie, like, but you're gonnae be OK. Yer ma and da are up. They're bidin wi' me and Roddy. Should be here ony minute. They're jist spikkin tae yer grunny on 'e phone. 'E docs thought they might hae tae amputate yer feet, which wis a bittie tricky cos your ma brought slippers for ye. But dinnae worry, I managed tae persuade 'e boy in 'e next bed tae buy 'em aff ye if 'e worst came tae 'e worst. Dave's offshore, but he's askin for ye. I've spoken tae Carol. She's glad you're still alive but she says she's gonnae murder you onywey for bein such an eejit."

"Eh was… surfin, eh?"

"Dinnae ken. Probably. They found you wye oot at sea."

"Neh board, though?"

"Na."

"Good."

"Really. Fit aboot California and Hawaii and Peru?"

"That wis aw shite. Eh dinneh think eh can ehven surf, rehlleh… Except eh mehbeh managed it thehr… Canneh mehnd."

"So nae professional surfin career. Fit ye gonnae dae?"

"Eh meht go… teh tehcher trehnin college. That's what the Mermehd thinks eh should deh."

"One tea wi' four, and one wi' one. Biscuits there an' a'. Will we see if we can sit you up a bittie, Robert?"

# 40

He had passed a largely sleepless night with weird dreams. Something in the *geist* disturbed him. He had heard his father rising and going downstairs, dressed for the chilly bedroom conditions and joined him in the kitchen.

"Cuppae tea, son?"

"Aye, please, da."

"Bugger, nae milk."

"I'll nip oot. Onythin else?"

"Na, that'll dae us." His father gave him a tenner. "Keep 'e chynge, Bobby."

Hold the fucking front page! "Cheers, da. You sure?"

Outside, thick mist. The lament of the foghorn further off than in *temps perdu*. From behind a privet hedge, she emerged and blocked his path. "We need to talk."

"OK. Keep an eye on 'e hoose, and when my Da's awa, come on in. I'll be back fae 'e shop in five minutes and I'll mak you some scran. Sound a'right?"

"Brilliant, Bobby. You never let me down, eh?"

Eggs, rowies, streaky bacon, sausages, Kellogg's Variety Pack, croissants, tattie scones, butter, jam, coffee, kippers, fruit and coo juices. Bob had never been a great chef, but following Roddy's departure for work after a hasty cuppa and Uglina's arrival, he had excelled himself. A world-class breakfast.

Quite how a way-below-average-size-eleven-year-old had managed to get outside the quantity of food she had done that morning was a mystery. Dave would have struggled to keep up. "Christ, how long since you last ate?"

"A few days, week maybe."

There had been no conversation during the feeding frenzy. Bob made himself a coffee and sat down opposite her at the kitchen table.

"Brian Bruce."

"The policeman?"

"Aye. Deserves some credit and he winnae get it unless you do him a favour."

"Didnae think you liked the polis. Elucidate."

"He might have saved somebody's life. You might ken who it is. Naebody else except me does. We need to find him."

They had made their way down to the beach. Hard to see your hand in front of your face so close to the sea. On the prom, she had stopped. "He'll just be up there."

"Dinnae tell me. You're observant."

"And bright and resourceful. You're on your own." And she vanished like magic into the fog.

In the next shelter along, perhaps the very one where they had wrestled back in the day, PC Bruce once again reeked up a smoke as Bob joined him. "Tae fit dae I owe 'e pleasure 'is time?"

"Unidentified victim ay some kind, I believe. Dinnae ken, but I've been telt I may be able tae help."

A car had been summoned. Unclear to Bob where they were heading, but his money was on the morgue, a maritime incident and the Silver Surfer. Two out of three ain't bad. They had made their way up to Intensive Care. A pink staff nurse had assured them that mortal danger was past and that he would be back on the ward later that day.

"I need tae mak some phone calls." The Panda car had still been waiting and ferried them down to Grampian Police HQ. Brian had commandeered an office and completed a report while Bob enjoyed the novelty of being an imaginary detective. It had seemed important, counter-intuitively, to phone the Langstane Press first. For the first time in his life, he told his father everything. It took an hour, the longest conversation they had ever had. In return, hospitality was offered at McMillan Acres to anyone that needed it.

Next, not for the first time, he had woken Carol up after a night shift, spreading inordinate joy and acquiring a Tayside phone number which he had subsequently rung.

# 41

## 1956

*The Blackboard Jungle*. That film changed everything. As the opening credits rolled and Bill Haley played, the cinema was on its feet. She'd been back to see it three times just for that buzz. And then, from Nashville via the cargo ships that docked in Glasgow, "Heartbreak Hotel", followed by the pictures of the guy singing it. "Wow!" From another, impossibly sexy planet. For the kids at the pink granite art school in Schoolhill this was all the inspiration they ever needed. For the general citizenry of Aberdeen the impact was negligible. Her brother George and his mate Roddy got it though, and through Maggie's imaginative and resourceful clothes shopping and alterations and improvised barbering skills they made a fair stab at the look, and were roundly mocked for it. She was delighted with her role as Dr. Frankenstein and painted them to the satisfaction of some of her tutors.

Everyone had had it tough. Born in the depression and raised in a small dull grey chilly world of rationing in a small dull grey chilly city was all she ever knew and as such it hadn't seemed so bad. At least they weren't getting bombed as bad as the poor folk in Clydebank, Coventry and the East End.

What made life intolerable was her parents. Rev. Fraser and his wife served a joyless God, had no real friends apart from his brother and his wife, another minister who lived in Perth, out of the same stable. For a naturally gregarious girl, the only release apart from fighting with her big brother came at Mile End Primary School, where, despite conspicuous academic underachievement, she drew everything, and somehow managed to be accepted at Aberdeen Academy. From the front entrance you could see Gray's College of Art across the road and the students and lecturers coming and going about their improbably glamorous business. It was her only ambition, and despite an absolute parental veto she pursued it ruthlessly.

When it came to the crunch, it was eviction from the family home or art school and there was no contest. She moved into a wee flat in Hutcheon Street by herself and somehow managed to survive on her student grant and a meagre scholarship. Feeling out of her depth among the urbane sophisticates, she knuckled down and worked like a slave for two years. During this time she got good, and she got popular. She was a bonny lass, friendly, straightforward and down-to-earth in a world of poseurs. She had never had time before, but, in the summer between her second and third years, after signing the portrait of the two proto-rockers, she was approached by Roddy McMillan, then a trainee printer, who offered to take her out. She accepted, and they stepped out every weekend. Roddy embraced his new image, and they became faces about town.

But there had always been Jimmy MacKay. On the first day at Gray's their eyes had met across the room and a foregone conclusion occurred. Jimmy, or Seamus, to be exact, was from Wester Ross and another square peg in the art school milieu. With the best will in the world, he couldn't really paint or sculpt to save himself, but he loved to take photos, and he was really good at that, and his self-deprecating wit and sardonic world-view made her laugh. The fact that he looked like Eddie Cochran in *The Girl Can't Help It* also endeared him to her. In any breaks they had, they would gravitate towards one another, and if he was free, he would sit quietly and watch her painting. She wouldn't have let anyone else do this. Likewise, she would help him in the darkroom. As they watched one another's magic develop, the sexual chemistry was working as well as the photographic.

Jimmy had decided to stay in Aberdeen that summer rather than head back to the west coast, and one sunny August Tuesday when, unheard of for Aberdeen, it was too hot to do anything, they took the tram out to Garthdee and walked out along the river. Finding themselves on Stewartie's Island, they unpacked their picnic. Jimmy had brought a bottle of Italian wine, rare as hens' teeth in fifties Ab. Maggie had never drunk before, but they were in amongst rabbits, a hedgehog, deer, nature in all its splendour and not another soul in sight and it just seemed right. After the wine he got the camera out and suggested they recreate Millais's "Ophelia." Under the influence of the prevailing spell, she laid down in the cool shallow water at the bank of the Dee, her white dress now transparent as Jimmy snapped away.

She protested as he took off her wet clothes, but the wine inhibited the inhibitions, and she found herself unable to resist. He was slight, but surprisingly strong, and there was nothing she could do about the... what was it? Rape, she supposed, though she didn't really know what was happening down there on the moss. Not fun any more, that was for sure. They made their way back on the clanking tram, Maggie in silence, Jimmy professing his undying love.

A month later, the sickness started. During that month, Jimmy had been attentive, apologetic and a degree of normal relations had been re-established. At weekends she still hit the town with Roddy. Had she not been suffering so badly, she would never have done it, but she couldn't cope on her own, returned to the family home and her mother took her straight to the doctor's. The diagnosis was swift, devastating and exactly what Mrs. Fraser expected, having been that soldier not once but twice. Maggie was confined to barracks, but allowed out for a walk down to Westburn Park. Where she met Jimmy every day. He proposed marriage, but the trust had gone. When it was announced, however, that she was to be sent to her aunt and uncle in Perth, he promised to give up art school and join her there. Her exit from Gray's and the Granite City was unannounced to Roddy. He only found out later through Dod, who assumed the relationship with Roddy McMillan was the motive and remained as ignorant of the true situation as the rest of the world.

As they piled into the Popular and headed south, Jimmy threw his bags on the train and started a new life as the *Dundee Courier's* photographer in Perth, living in digs by the St. Johnstone football ground at Muirton. The work was ill-paid but undemanding, and he continued to meet Maggie every day to relieve the crushing boredom they both felt, substituting the North Inch for Westburn Park as autumn turned to winter to spring. In the evenings he went to the Old Ship Inn on the High Street to continue the boredom relief where he spent his wages on a rapidly-developing relationship with booze and supplemented them by becoming adept at cheating in the nightly poker game.

And the day came in May when she didn't show, being otherwise engaged at Perth Royal Infirmary. Kirsty was 7 lbs. and healthy. Jimmy took his lunchtime sandwich faithfully to the banks of the Tay, and one day, she was there with a pram. He thought his heart was going to explode, and once again he proposed becoming Kirsty's daddy, but arrangements had already been made. The Mitchells were childless parishioners of Maggie's uncle and had met and fallen in love with the wee lassie. They were comfortably off and she would be adored and cared for. It had not been presented to Maggie as a choice. Phone calls from Aberdeen had made this patently clear. As a hopeless gesture he bought the bairn a rag doll the next day. She seemed to love it.

Within a week the deed was done, and the grey Ford arrived to take Maggie back. Jimmy stayed on. She hadn't told her parents who the father was, but knew that if he was on the scene, they would work it out and the situation would be unbearable. Part of her still loved him dearly, but loved what might have been rather than what was.

Meanwhile, with time on his hands, Jimmy MacKay spent a lot of time in the Mitchells' neighbourhood hoping to catch a glimpse of his daughter. Sometimes he even summoned up the courage to stop Mrs. Mitchell with the pram and pass the time of day with them, and, he noted, the rag doll, but it was hopeless. Otherwise, with nothing to do at lunchtimes any more, he would find himself doing an extra shift in the boozer. Then one Saturday he went to the off-licence at chucking-out time, bought a big cairry-oot, and spent the afternoon by the river drinking it until five o'clock rolled around, and an important line had been crossed.

He still worked, though, and indeed picked up extra doing weddings, property photos, portraits, even some calendar shots.

Still lovesick, he returned to Aberdeen one weekend in search of his erstwhile soulmate. She wasn't so hard to find. Simply a question of hanging out by her father's church on a Sunday. She hardly recognised him, with the beergut and the bad skin, but slipped away while her parents were distracted with parishioners' business and they wandered down and took a seat on the grass slope of Foresterhill.

"How are you, Jimmy?"

"You see it all. Keeping busy, like. How about yersel, Maggie? Still painting?"

"No, nae since… I'm OK, though. You seen Kirsty?

"Ay, now and again. She's fine. Getting to be a big girl."

I'm gettin merrit."

"Whit?"

"Ay. Next wikkend. Me and Roddy. I'm sorry, Jimmy. We got back thegither. He disnae ken, before you ask. He jist thinks I was sent awa cos my parents didnae approve ay him. Which they dinnae, by the way. But they've kindae given up on me. I think they reckon onythin's better than nithin. Christ, fit a guddle it is organisin a weddin. C'mere, you dinnae ken ony photographers, dae ye? A'body seems tae be booked up for Setterday."

"I'll do it."

"Fit?"

"I said I'll do it. For free. If you're stuck."

"Dinnae think 'at's a good idea, Jimmy."

"Why no? Promise I'll behave myself."

And, before they parted, he managed to convince her of his proficiency, availability and willingness and the deal was reluctantly done. He would see her back at the church on Saturday. He repaired to the Atholl Hotel on King's Gate for the lunchtime sesh, sat down with a pint and a dram and reviewed the situation.

He was just about making a survival income with the photography, but it was taking a fair dunt from the booze, and that was now non-negotiable. He needed a new source of income. Over the next couple of hours a bold plan was formulated. He jumped on a tram downtown and thence onto the Glasgow train, tipsily satisfied with his day's work.

Jimmy took care to remain incognito at the marriage. You could tell Rev. Fraser was spitting, but he got through the afternoon with the best grace he could in the circumstances, short of actually smiling for the camera. Back at the Atholl Hotel, Jimmy laid off the sauce reasonably successfully and took some great pics, in his own humble opinion. As other people danced, the minister sat alone at a table and the time had come.

He got himself a large whisky and took a seat. Back in Achnasheen he'd dealt with the Wee Frees. The regular Church of Scotland needed hold no terrors. Small potatoes. No sense in beating about the bush. "I know, Reverend Fraser, about the child."

"What child?"

"The wee girl, in Perth. There's no point in denying it. I know everything. Here's what I propose. Every first Sunday of the month, I will go to your brother's morning service. At the end of the service, I will approach him outside, and he will hand me an envelope containing £100. If not, what you have tried to conceal will become common knowledge."

"I don't know what you're havering about, young man."

"As you wish. This would seem as good a place to start spreading the word as any." And he rose.

"Sit down!" The minister tried to horse trade on the sum, but Jimmy stuck to his guns. When the deal was concluded, his proferred handshake was declined, but the agreement was there, and as June turned into July, he sat near the Mitchells at church in Perth, and at the end of the service enquired whether the younger Rev. Fraser had the envelope and was handed it without question.

Every so often he would go up to Aberdeen and engineer a

chance meeting with Maggie when he could. Jeez, you only had to look at her, it seemed. Almost nine months to the day from the wedding and there were twins, Katherine and Robert. She looked well, happy, he thought, made it clear that Seamus MacKay was to have no part in the lives of the new-borns, but still needed to see him as the only link to wee Kirsty.

The years went by and he took to going to the kirk every Sunday. He saw his daughter and cultivated the friendship of the Mitchell family, but he was too pished too often, and this, coupled with the minister's discouragement, led to an estrangement between them. He still watched her development from a distance, though, and was there as she turned up, doll still in hand, for her first day of school.

# 42

## 1968

The years flew by, and each Sunday in church he saw her grow, bonny and dark, the spit of her mum. He had spoken to her a couple of times, giving nothing away, of course, but the Mitchells disapproved. As a fellow churchgoer he still had some meagre social interaction with them, however, had managed to give the impression that Jesus was on his side in his struggle with the demon drink while still ensuring that the children of the Old Ship Inn's publican would never go hungry, and one Sunday, gave them a breezy "See you next week" on leaving the kirk, only to be informed that he wouldn't. It was the summer holidays before Kirsty went to secondary school and Mrs. Mitchell told him they were to spend the next weekend in Aberdeen.

Jimmy speculated wildly. Had the elder Rev. and Mrs. Fraser relented and now wished to meet and perhaps even acknowledge their grand-daughter? Was Maggie to be involved in some way? Either way this had a possible bearing on his income and he resolved to monitor the situation closely. He was now the proud owner of a used Austin 1100 which remained parked, with a travelling bag packed, in the Mitchells' street most of that week. He didn't even drink until the evenings. A couple of close calls, but he was fairly sure he avoided discovery, and on the Friday, when the Rover filled up with bags and pulled away from the driveway of the Mitchell residence, he eased into gear and tailed them at a safe distance. His conjecture had involved them perhaps lodging at the old Fraser place, but he was relieved to see them pull up at a guest house in Ferryhill. He was tempted to let Maggie know somehow, but no, this was business. Having arranged to stay with a couple of old art school pals, he met them in Ma Cameron's and a riotous evening ensued, during which he almost convinced them of his credentials as Perth's answer to David Bailey.

Despite the hangover, he was up early the next morning and got to Ferryhill just in time to continue the surveillance job. The sun shone but a stiff breeze blew as he tailed them down to the beach. A stripey windbreak was erected preserving the modesty of the Mitchell family as they changed into swimming gear and gallantly took the plunge. Must have been fucking freezing and they didn't last long. Kirsty, still with the doll despite her advanced age, was vigorously towelled dry by Mrs M.

Nothing to see here, and Jimmy made his way to the Inversnecky Café for a coffee to kick start his fuzzy heid. On his exit, he was confronted by two bath chairs passing in front of the establishment. Hoping against hope that they didn't do likewise, he immediately recognised their occupants. The Rev. and Mrs. Fraser looked old and ill. They were pushed by a couple who looked as decrepit as they did. Part of his flock, perhaps? Was it coincidence or was he not the only undercover operative here? But they didn't even look down at the beach, or at him, their minds seemingly focused on the faraway Beach Ballroom and the manifold sins committed therein, or on eternity perhaps?... He hadn't really contemplated how he would cope when his cash cow died. They passed by and he leaned over the railing and watched the Mitchells.

Mr. M was back in his street clothes and making his way up the steps from the sand. Jimmy withdrew a little along the prom and watched him enter the café. Down on the beach Kirsty, doll still in hand, had climbed up on to one of the wooden groynes and was inching her way gingerly along it. As she got further out the structure became greener with algae. He applauded the wee girl's spirit. It was the kind of challenge he would have embraced as a wee boy.

And then she slipped as a wave hit her, and tumbled into the water. Could she swim? On her last visit to the sea she had only messed about in the shallows. Mrs. Mitchell had been watching her like a hawk, and what became immediately obvious was that *she* couldn't. She screamed as Kirsty surfaced, already considerably further out, and then disappeared again. Nobody else on the beach seemed to realise what had happened. Eventually a young lad took Mrs. M on, and after a brief exchange stripped off and swam out. Jimmy could see he was going the wrong way. He wanted to go to his daughter's rescue, but how could he explain his presence? He watched hopefully yet hopelessly. She never reappeared.

Mr. Mitchell, little suspecting the turn of events, returned to the sand to find his wife distraught and guilt-ridden. Other beachgoers gathered round and crowded them. A few more of them swam out, but to no avail. Police, coastguards and ambulances arrived. Also the fourth estate. As journalists and a photographer added to their misery, a lifeboat went back and forth more in aspiration than expectation. By late afternoon, all hope had been abandoned, and the beach gradually cleared.

When Mr. and Mrs. Mitchell eventually left, Jimmy MacKay sat down on the sand as the tide ebbed. Darkness began to close in and he strolled aimlessly along the tideline. It wasn't like he'd had any sort of relationship with the wee lassie. Still… Christ, he needed a drink right now. As he was considering which howff should get his business, a wave deposited something on the seaweed. In the gathering gloom, he couldn't make out what it was, but bent down and picked up the doll.

Back in Perth, what little *joie de vivre* he had possessed disappeared. Every day he took the *Press and Journal*, and soon, within two weeks of one another, he read the obituary notices of Mrs. and Rev. Fraser. No more Sundays in church, then. That was a relief, but a severe hit to the cashflow.

His work became haphazard. Often he would sit by the Tay with a bottle, always of spirits or sometimes tonic wine these days, rather than go out on a job, and it was no surprise when the phone call came relieving him of all responsibilities to the *Dundee Courier*. He had never really liked Perth anyway, and one day, he sold the car for a pittance and shared his bottle with a squad of Gordon Highlanders and Black Watch on the train back up to Aberdeen.

For a while he crashed on the couches of old student pals but quickly wore out his welcome, both with them, and soon also at the Salvation Army Citadel. He gravitated, however, to a community of like-minded individuals who helped him with survival tips.

About this time Margaret McMillan took a job as a sales assistant at Taylor's back on Schoolhill, Aberdeen's only artists' suppliers. Even after all these years, deep down there was a part of Roddy McMillan that could not believe Maggie had not left him yet, and he was always wary of upsetting her, but he protested. He was now making a decent whack as a printer at the Langstane Press, prided himself on being the breadwinner and did not feel the need for further household income. They had always argued about the family finances, Roddy living up to every Aberdonian stereotype, and Maggie made it clear that she was doing it for personal pocket money. The kids were now ten, and could make their own way to and from school, she needed to have a life outside the house. The truth was somewhat more bizarre.

One day, coming out of the family home, she was approached by a stranger.

"How you doing, Maggie?" He was in rags, badly needed a haircut and shave, his speech was slurred and he stank. "Or would it help if I said 'Ciamar a tha thu, Maighréad'?"

"Christ, Jimmy, that's never you, is it? What's happened?

"Fallen on hard times, darling. A concatenation of circumstances, as they say."

"Jeez, anything I can do to help?"

"Now you mention it, there is. I tend to be at the Castlegate a lot of the time. If you could meet me, let's say outside Esslemont and Macintosh at one o'clock every Saturday and give me £20 that would be marvellous."

"I dinnae hiv that sortae money, Jimmy."

"I take it your family don't know about Kirsty?"

"Kirsty's deid. That story's finished."

"Is it, though? Nobody knows for sure. They never found a body, I believe. Be that as it may, I'm sure your husband would be delighted to know about our life together in Perth."

"Fit life thegither? We had no life thegither."

"We had a child, Maggie. How can you say we had no life together? It would be your word against mine."

"And it would be your word against mine if I was to go to the police and report a sexual assault."

"But I don't think you're going to do that, are you? No, I know you too well. So, I can wait here till your kids get home from school and Roddy gets home from work, or we can come to a civilised arrangement and your life will continue as normal."

And so it was concluded and, though he said so himself, Seamus

MacKay had become rather good at this.

Back at the Castlegate among his new gang, Jimmy knew better than to brag about his change of fortune. He enjoyed the reckless life of the full-time alkie and the camaraderie that came with it. Months passed into years in a haze, but it never got old. Outsiders could criticise, but there was always something crazy and amusing happening and the squares could fuck right off. For instance, Scary Ivy, despite years of bodily abuse, was now obviously pregnant and the word was that the Professor, who apparently had been an actual professor of philosophy at Aberdeen University, was the father.

One day she collapsed in pain, and when even industrial spirits had no effect, Jimmy called 999. A child, Alison, was delivered, astonishingly healthy, and the decision to take the wee girl into care was one of the easiest Social Services ever had to make.

# 43

## 1979

Her life in the institution was miserable, punctuated by cruelty and neglect. The only kindness, from a couple of older men on the staff, toys, compliments, sweeties and also booze which she found nauseating and refused, rang alarm bells that others may not have heard and she kept herself safe. She read voraciously when she could. Anything. Stories, atlases, encyclopaedias, animal and bird books, she took refuge in the realm of the imagination. She was a bright, resourceful kid, and as such was classed as a disruptive child, a bad influence on the others. She learnt to live with it, but, at the age of eleven, she had also learnt from watching the TV that there was a better life out there. She loved the detective shows that she sometimes got to watch in the staff room after bedtime, "Hazell" and "The Sweeney", and basing her technique on them, determined to find out who her parents were. She managed to break into the filing cabinet in the office and read her dossier. And there they were, Ivy Tocher and John Colquhoun. But who were they, where were they? She was informed, further down, that she had been taken into care on account of their alcoholism. From her avid viewing, she had some understanding of what this meant, but no idea where a person might find alcoholics in Aberdeen. The dinner ladies she asked were surprised and amused, but under forceful interrogation eventually volunteered that she should probably start at the Castlegate.

"About this time, something went weird with ma heid, and it all jist seemed unreal, it seemed like everything wis falling apart. I did some terrible things, ken. I set fire to my heid. I wis attention-seeking, except I dinnae really think that's true, cos as soon as I'd done it I didnae want anybody to ken cos I wis really embarrassed. I just wanted to destroy myself and for naebody to remember that I'd ever existed. And then this other quine took the pish out ay me and I got in a fight with her, but I didnae want to hurt her really, it wis like I wanted her to hurt me. Anyway, it wis a pretty mental fight, and I got so angry that she wisnae really hurting me that I hurt her. Wi' a bottle. And I got social and psychiatric reports and I didnae do very well in them. Then everybody was dead nice to me for a change, but they werenae for real. When one ay the older lassies topped herself, I kent I had to dae the same or get out and dae what normal people dae, nae ither alternatives."

One chilly Sunday, at the end of their outing to church, she slipped away. Forever. Simple as that. Following the directions of strangers, she found herself free at the bottom of Union Street, confronted by a hairy, smelly man sitting on the steps of the Mercat Cross, consuming a Camping Gaz refill.

"Are you an alcoholic?"

"Cheeky wee hooer."

"No, but are you? I need to know."

"I'm no gonnae lie to you. I do enjoy a drink."

"I'm going to ask you one more time. Are you an alcoholic?"

"Jesus. You're a right wee ballbreaker, eh? OK, my name is, wait a minute, Seamus, aye, Seamus MacKay and I am an alcoholic."

"Great. Do you know Ivy Tocher and John Colquhoun?"

"Seems to ring a bell. Aye, Scary Ivy, and the Professor's name was Colquhoun, I believe. Well, I did. They're deid now, like."

"Deid?"

"Aye."

"How did they die?"

"How does anybody round here die. You just find them in the morning, usually. Dinnae cry, darling, Ivy and the Professor werenae really people it's worth greeting about. I had a daughter once. She died. Looked a wee bit like you. Now that's worth a few tears. Who are you, anyway?"

"I'm anonymous, Seamus."

"Right. I'm gonnae call you Kirsty. What are you daeing here? Where's your Ma and Da?"

"They're deid."

"Where do you stay?"

"As of today, nowhere. Can I trust you?"

"No. But I can make sure you survive. That's one thing I know how to do."

And Jimmy was as good as his word. Though often cold and hungry, the wee girl never froze or starved, and avoided the authorities. In return, he came to rely on her to an extent. She was discreet, smelt polis and do-gooders from a mile off, could twist people round her little finger, had an uncanny knack of getting what they needed and they became a team. One day he produced the bedraggled rag doll from an inside pocket like the relic of a saint and said he wanted her to have it. Alison was sensitive enough to realise that she was a surrogate for his dead daughter, accepted the gift, and kept it with her. To pass long desperate days when he had no drink he continued to observe the McMillan family from a distance, but only met Maggie now to pick up the money every week. Despite the promised undying love that still burnt hidden somewhere deep in his soul there was no further interaction, but he wanted to keep abreast of the situation, if only to see if there was any more leverage to be had. He assigned the surveillance job to the wee girl, encouraging her to get to find out about them if she could. She could, and soon came back with news of Kathy living in Peterhead with two bairns, and then of her husband's walk-out, and of Bobby's life at Edinburgh University and his eventual return. The spymaster had made it clear that Mrs. McMillan must never see the doll, and advised his *protegée* to concentrate on Robert.

# 44

## 1980

RADADA RADADA| DA DA DAA DA| DADADADA DA
DA| DA
DADA| DA, DADA DA, DADA| DA DA DA,
DADA| DA, DADA DA, DADA| DA DA DA DADA|
DA DA DA DADA| DA DA DA
DADA |DAA DAA DA|A DADADADADA

It's where they had all learnt simple syncopation, Roddy as a trumpeter, Kathy as a clarinettist, Bobby as a violinist. The bond was unspoken, but from the Austro-Hungarian Imperialist chocolate box, the Radetzky March united them.

He had risen unseasonably early for no reason. No sense to it at all. Even beat Liam and Alice to it. He donned a dressing gown and repaired to the bathroom to deal with the natural start to the day, went down to the kitchen, boiled a kettle, lit a fire and switched the TV on for the anticipated arrival of the kids in the sitting room and took a cup of tea back to his bedroom. It had been a good Hogmanay, with Kathy and the bairns down from the Blue Toon, and visits after the bells from Dod and his Auntie Ann and from Dave and Kim, notable for a Talisker-induced thawing of the chill between him and his father. They had even made one another laugh. The younger generation had gone out to a party later but hadn't stayed too long or got *too* pished. He reached for the drawer of his bedside table and removed an old *P and J*.

ABERDEEN LIFEBOAT IN LATE-NIGHT DRAMA
Cox says rescue was million to one chance

And a dead-of-night picture of the crew grinning floodlit outside the boathouse, teas in one hand, thumbs-up with the other.

As a piece of artistic punctuation to the Old Year, he decided to visit the scene of the crime. Crossing the links with his hands in his jacket pockets, he discovered the wee square of blotting paper the Monkey had given him. Probably past its sell-by date, but he necked it for the sake of tidiness and wished Johnny Barr a Happy New Year. So, wild, wild winter day at the beach. He leaned for ages on the prom railing in what would have been the shadow of the Penguin Baths if there had been any sun. Was he feeling a wee bit trippy? He wasn't sure. Across the links, the magic of Pittodrie lay ghostly quiet, the Ne'er Day game postponed this year. In Sandy Bollocks's damning review, the Penguin Baths featured unfavourably. It was a seawater pool housed in a spectacularly unattractive piece of architecture. And not noticeably warmer than the sea itself. The advantage the North Sea had was the reduced risk of swallowing used Elastoplast. Today the waves were fierce. The tide almost covered the whole beach, and spindrift drenched him with every breaker.

The very last day you would choose for a seaside excursion, and yet a few hardy weird-looking dogs and their weird-looking walkers passed him on the prom.

Definitely getting something off it now. He watched the stone-age TV till, down on the beach itself, there she was. With the doll. She did not look in his direction, but mounted the nearest concrete platform, skipped down and ventured out onto the wooden groyne, already almost completely submerged. She walked out purposefully, seemingly oblivious to the danger, for some twenty yards, then turned, smiled sadly and made the doll wave once again at Bob. Goodbye, not hello, it seemed to him, as a huge wave broke and swept her under.

The dilemma was clear-cut. Any attempt at rescue would come

at serious risk to his own survival. Also, the look she had given him in that last moment had spoken volumes. She looked calm, as if she knew exactly what she was doing, and it was what she intended. As he scanned the waves, though, she resurfaced and with surprising strength, made it back to the structure with a mad doggy paddle, pulled herself out of Aberdeen Bay, standing on the groyne made eye contact with Bob again and flung the doll as far out to sea as she could. As she did so a disreputable figure arrived at drunken speed along the narrow strip of beach, threw off his jacket and plunged into the surf. No mistaking him. The erstwhile classicist and hairspray *aficionado* swam out to roughly the point where the doll had vanished and vanished himself, never to re-emerge. Bob did not even entertain the concept of a stab at a rescue in this case as Uglina tightroped back to the beach and ran off towards the Bridge of Don.

He was dubious as to the extent of Norrin's knowledge of the Aberdeen beach currents, but recent events did seem to back up his theory. Despite the wind getting stronger and the sea wilder, he descended the steps to the sand. Fuckin freezing! Blown spume off Hokusai waves soaked him. Off the top of a huge breaker, a surfboard was flung onto the beach. He did not need to inspect it closely, and sat where he was, for who knows how long, before deciding to leave it where it was. Just as he admitted defeat to the weather and decided to head to the Viennese/old-movie, open-fire warmth of home, he noticed another item of debris deposited by the now-receding tide. He rose and, at the water's edge, picked up the sodden doll.

# EPILOGUE

Surprisingly, he slept well. He was awoken by the guard bringing him the proverbial hearty breakfast. As he ate, there was activity outside the door, respectfully lowered voices. His reputation still counted for something. There were those who believed he had done what he had done as a patriotic duty, to restore democracy to the republic. He had played his cards close to his chest.

As he drained the last of his coffee the key turned and an armed guard stood ready. As he rose he returned their salute. Whatever he had become, he had been, in a varied and distinguished career, General Kim, commander of the Third Army Group. As such, he marched smartly down the corridor with his escort. He caught the eyes of one of the young soldiers, wondered what the future held for him, for all the people, North and South.

The door at the end of the passage opened in anticipation. Without a reason why, he had expected more of a show, more people, a larger room at least. It was totally dominated by the trap-doored platform. He slowly climbed the steps, eyeing the rope. Everything looked ship-shape. The burly man holding the hood was impassive. Kim Jae-Gyu had played chess with the Grim Reaper before and won. Not this time.